Bertha Bartlett Public Library

DATE DUE

SE 14 '00			
SE 27 '00			
OC 5 '00			
NO 3 '00			
DE 1 '00			
DE 12 '00			
JA 2 '01		WITHDRAWN	
JA 13 '01			
MAY 6 2003			
JAN 2 1 2004			
MAR 6 2004			
CP 6·08			
Cedar 7-1-11			
6-22-12			
AG 04 '11			
(8) 2015			

DEMCO 38-297

BERTHA BARTLETT PUBLIC LIBRARY
503 Broad St.
Story City, IA 50248

CASEY'S JOURNEY

CASEY'S JOURNEY

•

Marjorie M. McGinley

AVALON BOOKS
NEW YORK

© Copyright 2000 by Marjorie M. McGinley
Library of Congress Catalog Card Number: 00-190024
ISBN 0-8034-9421-1
All rights reserved.
All the characters in this book are fictitious,
and any resemblance to actual persons,
living or dead, is purely coincidental.
Published by Thomas Bouregy & Co., Inc.
160 Madison Avenue, New York, NY 10016

PRINTED IN THE UNITED STATES OF AMERICA
ON ACID-FREE PAPER
BY HADDON CRAFTSMEN, BLOOMSBURG, PENNSYLVANIA

To Michael, Jr., Kristie, Douglas, Jr., Matthew and Joseph

Chapter One

The small fire at his campsite in the isolated red rock canyon was well hidden in the patch of scrubby juniper bushes, Tom Casey thought; so the rustling noise in the junipers and then the unwanted voice calling out to him from out there in the darkness beyond his view caused Casey to tense rapidly.

Glancing quickly down, he could see his Spencer rifle next to his right thigh, and his black leather gun belt with its "Confederate Colt" near his left hip on the brown, white, and red saddle blanket he was seated on.

"Hello the fire," the voice said again.

Only then did Tom answer, and cautiously.

"Come on in," he said, very reluctantly, the annoyance in his voice obvious if anyone was listening carefully.

The medium-height, heavily muscled man with disheveled, shiny, curly black hair came forward slowly

1

into the small amount of light that came from the very small fire.

Tom realized then he should have taken more seriously the advice of a crotchety old man named Whitey.

Whitey owned the last trading post Tom had stopped at. He'd advised Tom not to make a fire out here.

"But if you do make one, make it small . . . and hide it well," he'd said.

Whitey had said that the area Tom was heading toward in this section of northwestern Arizona Territory was one of danger, both from Indians and from "ruffians," as he'd called them. He meant robbers, Tom had guessed.

Tom swore inwardly to himself. *Dang!* Whitey was right; it was undoubtedly the small red glow of the fire that had attracted this stranger.

Tom squinted his eyes to get a better look at the intruder, who had come forward into the light and was standing there, seeming not to know what to do next.

Tom was irritated. Why had the man come to his camp at night? Why not make his own campfire? Was this stranger alone, or was someone else waiting out there in the darkness, ready to shoot Tom in the back?

Tom knew he made a good target and was very vulnerable surrounded as he was by darkness. They could see him but he couldn't see who or what was out there.

The man who showed himself at the edge of the light was a few years older than Tom. Tom had turned twenty-five on June 22, 1868, exactly one month ago.

Casey's Journey

The stranger came in closer and the first thing he noticed was that the man wore ill-fitting clothing that was different from what Tom was used to seeing, either back home in Virginia or here in the West.

"Might I be sittin' down?" the man finally inquired, and Tom nodded noncommittally. Although not openly hostile and unwelcoming, he hoped he was at least clearly indicating his displeasure at the stranger's sudden appearance at his remote campsite.

Tom, exhausted, had been planning on going right to sleep. And 9:00 was late to be appearing at a man's fire out of nowhere.

That plan—sleeping—was out of the question now.

The man ignored Tom's hostility, and sat himself down as if he was a happily welcomed guest or friend.

That, in itself, was somewhat additionally annoying.

Adjusting himself on the ground to make himself more comfortable, the stranger slid his hand under his leg to remove a small chunk of red sandstone rock in the sandy soil which he threw off to the side. Then he settled down.

The man raised his eyebrows questioningly and looked eagerly toward Tom's battered blue enamel coffeepot. Once again, Tom nodded reluctantly, and the man produced a battered tin cup from somewhere in his baggy clothing and wadded up the red-and-white cotton bandanna that Tom had left near the fire as a pot holder, and used it to pour coffee into his cup as if it were the most natural thing in the world.

The newcomer sipped the hot coffee, once again his eyebrows flicking up and down expressively as if to indicate how good the coffee was.

"Name is Peake," the man said after the first few swallows. "James Peake."

A few seconds passed.

"Slim Casey," Tom said reluctantly.

"Ah," the man said. "Irish, are ya." He breathed an obvious sigh of relief.

It was then that Tom noticed the man wore what his mother called brogans—sturdy, brown leather shoes such as he supposed people wore in Ireland and other foreign places. This man's were old, scuffed and worn, and a different style from American brogans.

His black, dusty clothing looked hand sewn, and was way too big on him, and the style was certainly not what a man around here—and for a very long distance around—would wear.

That explained the man's odd outfit and the accent. He was from Ireland.

He had a fairly pleasant looking face, and it was hard to be sure in the dim light, but Tom thought that he had blue eyes.

But Tom wanted to set him straight and distance himself from the clutches of this man who was acting much too familiar much too soon. Probably fresh out of Ireland.

"My family has been here for almost a hundred years," Tom said stiffly. "Came over before the Revolution."

The man was suddenly silent; he knew he had been rebuked.

There was silence for what seemed like a long time.

That was the way Tom wanted it, intended it, in fact. He wanted nothing but for this man to leave.

Now. He had enough problems right now without dealing with a . . . an oddly dressed, foreign stranger.

Tom was determined not to break the silence, or let his guard down. He himself was a stranger to this red rock area. He didn't necessarily want this stranger to know it, or indeed, any of his business.

The truth was, he'd never been this far west before.

"I don't suppose you'd be knowin'," the heavyset man said, chuckling ironically to himself as if he'd told himself a great joke, "bein' that your family has been away from the ol' sod so long, what your name means."

"Tom? Thomas?" Tom said. *Dang!* He'd inadvertently revealed his real name. He cursed himself for a fool; he was still no good at this "hiding things" stuff. Keeping secrets.

"No. Casey," the Irishman continued. "I don't suppose yer sainted mother or father ever told you what it means."

The man had accented the word "sainted" just the tiniest bit, knowing how to do it just enough so that Tom detected the ironic quality about it, but not openly enough so that Tom could bring himself to be offended by it.

The man had a clever way with words. And he was letting Tom know that he had noticed Tom's slightly superior attitude.

Tom thought for a moment. He doubted if his mother or father ever knew what their family name meant, themselves. His whole family had somewhat distanced themselves from their Irish roots and considered themselves Virginia aristocracy—at least until the war. Sometime, somewhere, they had even become Protestants.

But tonight, right now, the older man sitting a short distance on Tom's right had a look on his face—not quite a smirk, but darn close to it, as if he was inwardly chuckling to himself.

"Would you be knowin' if the Caseys were an O'Casey or a MacCasey?"

Tom thought for a moment. He did know that. He remembered seeing the name O'Casey on some old papers that his father had in his office on the plantation in Virginia, before that part of the house—the office—was destroyed by fire during the War Between the States. It was still a source of grief to him that the plantation house had been set on fire by the Yankees; it was a beautiful structure modeled after Thomas Jefferson's home at Monticello.

He was bitter about a lot of things. For one thing, he was angry about his mother's attitude about the war. The war that he'd heard that his very proper mother could only bring herself to call "The Late Unpleasantness." In spite of what it had done to her four sons and husband, and everyone around her. Especially to Ben, her third son.

"O'Casey," Tom said.

"Ah, just as I thought. Casey comes from the word *cathasach*."

"What does that mean?" Tom asked.

The Irishman sat there, enjoying the moment. Payback for Tom's reluctant hospitality and previous remark, Tom thought.

Well, maybe I deserve that, Tom said to himself.

The man chuckled, then he spoke, taking his time about it. "Watchful," he finally said. "Seems apparent the name fits, judging by your actions. Your family name means 'watchful.' "

"A man not careful out here can come to a quick end," Casey said defensively, leaning forward to put another very small piece of dead juniper branch on the fire.

The stranger nodded agreement. "All too true. All too true, I'm afraid."

But the man had captured Tom's interest: the name Casey meant "watchful" in Irish or Gaelic or Celtic or whatever you called the language of Ireland. His own ancestors had come from there a long time ago before settling and building up the large successful plantation on the Virginia shore east of Richmond.

He thought suddenly about his mother. She would have stuck up her nose at the wrinkled clothing this man was wearing.

If she'd instructed her servants to give this man a free meal, by his clothing alone she would have decided that he eat it out back, outside, hidden from view from the mansion. So she didn't have to see him.

She was a woman who had liked things clean and neat in her life. She liked her world to be pretty, kind and genteel. The world of polite Virginia society.

That world had come to a painful, permanent end and now Tom Casey was alone, camped for the night here in a canyon in the red rock country on an urgent mission. Exhausted. Drinking coffee with this annoyingly arrogant stranger.

And if the real truth be told, he didn't guess that he

looked any better than the man sitting near him at the fire. His own clothes were dusty and wrinkled, and it was a lot more than a day or two since he'd had water enough for a shave. His mother would have apoplexy if she knew that.

He'd traveled a long way today on his shiny, black, part-mustang gelding. Truthfully, too far, overtiring both himself and his small but powerful Western-bred horse.

Before the sun had set, he'd watered, fed, and curried his horse Blacky, who was picketed behind him. Thomas Logan Casey was tired and irritable.

He sighed.

The Irishman facing him, still wanting to talk, took no notice of how tired and sad Tom was.

Tom Casey had been raised to be painfully polite on the surface even to those he didn't like, so he sat there as the man said suddenly, "Your parents ever talk to you about brocking?"

Tom shook his head no. What the heck was brocking?

"Back on the ol' sod"—the man obviously meant Ireland—"if a man has more than one daughter, he wants to marry them off in order. The oldest is supposed to get married first, an' so on, down the line.

"Trouble is, sometimes the pretty one is the youngest. This can cause trouble, especially when a father or mother is stubborn and set in their ways."

Tom nodded. He could see the trouble that that could cause.

"Well, Daniel MacDermot of County Roscommon—where I come from—had five daughters.

Casey's Journey

"The two eldest, Nan and Bridey, were married off, but there was a problem after that. The third daughter—well, it is hard to find—"

And here Tom noticed that the Irishman seemed to choke up. He kept forging ahead with his story, but with a little emotional difficulty.

". . . well, 'tis hard to find something good to say about her. She was neither kind, nor a good cook, and was not pretty. Truthfully, you'd have to travel many an Irish mile to see a face . . . well, as bad as hers."

He thought a little more before he continued. "An' little, beady, close-together black eyes with a great overhangin' brow."

Here the Irishman grew silent. Then he added, "A tragic disfigurement, I guess you would call it."

He was silent so long that Tom wondered if the man was going to continue with the story at all.

Tom could see that James Peake was thinking—no, maybe reliving and picturing in his head something that had happened. He was lost in thought.

Finally, with a little start, Peake realized where he was and what he had previously said to Tom.

"Ach, sorry," the man said with his thick brogue. "Anyway, that third daughter, Pegeen, put a dead stop to the marriage prospects of the last two daughters, Maureen and Nellie.

"Sadly, it was just my fate to fall madly in love with the next daughter in line after ugly Pegeen. I was madly in love with Maureen, and I'm still not ashamed to say it and declare my love for her . . . at the time.

"Reddish-blond, shiny hair she had, and green eyes, just the tiniest sprinkling of soft freckles, and with the most beautiful smile that would melt a heart of marble. Kind too, nary a mean bone in her body. Not like ugly Pegeen a'tall.

"Three years it was, I waited for some poor soul to come along and ask for the hand of the unfortunate horse-faced Pegeen, figgerin' that some man—some poor unfortunate soul—would come along who was her equal in looks and temperament.

"Then Pegeen would be out of the way so that the next daughter's turn to marry might come. My own dear mother said that 'there's a shoe for every foot'—that in itself was a bit of a joke, as not that many of us even *had* shoes—but she meant that someone would come along for Pegeen. So I waited."

Tom had to admit to himself that this story was getting so interesting that he was no longer sleepy. He leaned forward and listened intently as Peake continued. Once in a while Peake took a sip of coffee as he spoke, and once he refilled his cup from the enamel coffeepot.

"Finally, Maureen and I—for I was so fortunate that Maureen returned the love I had for her—we got tired of waiting, and I was so bold as to ask her father—may his wicked soul burn forever in Hades—for the hand in matrimony of the beautiful Maureen."

When Peake said the words "burn forever in Hades," he made the sign of the cross on himself as if to ward off the vengeance of God for having said such a thing.

Then he continued, "Oddly enough, the old hooligan said yes right away.

"I should have suspected something right then . . .

Casey's Journey

but I figgered that he had come to the same conclusion that Maureen and I had: that Pegeen was a lost cause as far as marriage was concerned.

"On the day of the wedding, I was the happiest man in the whole of Ireland—whisht! maybe the whole world! In my joy I had forgotten a simple thing: that Maureen's father could sometimes be a man with odd thinking and, also, which I didn't know at the time, an evil heart.

"I never knew who it was, himself or Mrs. MacDermot, whose idea it was, but as the ceremony ended, when it came time for me to lift up the thick white veil and kiss the bride, you can imagine my shock to see it was not Maureen I had married a'tall!

"I was facing—forever married to—the horse-toothed, dreaded, nasty *Pegeen!*

"They had substituted Pegeen in Maureen's place, and I, and James Augustus Peake, was married to the meanest woman I had ever seen! Maybe the meanest woman ever put on earth!

"And what was I, if not a good Catholic, and no divorce allowed! Ever!

"They—Maureen's family—had tricked me! A vile, dirty trick!

"Worse, I don't know if Maureen was in on it or not. I hope not!

"But still, the truth is, Maureen never warned me. Never even snuck me the slightest warning. I'd noticed that I was not allowed to see Maureen alone before the wedding, always with her mother or someone else present. But that was not so unusual in our small, strict village."

Tom was shocked.

"What did you do?" Tom said.

"They might just as well have killed me that day. In a terrible way they did."

The Irishman sighed and was silent.

"But what did you do?" Tom asked again.

Chapter Two

"I turned on me heel and walked right on out of that church and never stopped walking west until I reached the harbor at Westport. There, I got on a ship and came to America—New York.

"I was just lucky that that day I had on me the money I'd saved for my wedding. For me and Maureen," he added bitterly.

"I can't believe that anyone—a family—would do a terrible thing like that," Tom said.

"Neither could I," the Irishman said slowly and sadly.

Tom thought about the fact that the man next to him would be unable to marry ever again. He was trapped forever in that marriage.

"What happened to Maureen?" Tom asked.

"I never found out."

"Do you still care for her?"

"I don't think I will ever care for anyone. My heart has grown poisoned, bitter. Perhaps turned to stone."

The Irishman was silent.

Tom thought about the situation. James Peake had to live with the fact that he didn't know if Maureen was in on the plot. And she had not at least warned Peake about what was going to happen.

"That was a terrible thing that that family did to you, James."

"Call me Jim, please." Jim rubbed his forehead in despair.

"Sadly, that wasn't the end of it. I was in America two years, working on the Baltimore and Ohio Railroad, making a new life for meself, until one day a man from Roscommon got on a train and I recognized him. It was himself, Francis Dillon, a good friend of mine who was at the wedding.

"He told me that MacDermot's life had gone to ruin after what he did to me. Instead of blaming it on his own evil deed, for no one was trustin' him in business dealings after that, or wantin' anything to do with the whole lot of them, he blamed all his troubles on *me*. He paid two local men to come to America and to find and kill me.

"Francis Dillon told me that MacDermot thinks that if he kills me that all his troubles will be over."

"Is that why you ended up here?" Tom said.

"The man on the train, Dillon, said that MacDermot's men—the hired killers—had already got wind of the fact that I was working for the railroad.

"I figgered I had to make a run for it. I figgered if

Casey's Journey 15

I came West the two killers wouldn't be able to find me.

"My boss, a good man, managed to get me railway passes for as far as he could. Where me railway pass ended—Sedalia, Missouri—I got a job driving a freight wagon to Santa Fe.

"They called me a 'mule skinner'—I found out that's the name for men who drive a mule team—and heaven help me, I could have skinned a few of them ornery creatures!

"Had *more* than my share of run-ins with stubborn mules on the trail!

"Whisht! Those mule skinners could cuss! An' what's worse, after a while I couldn't blame them!" He shook his head in wonderment.

Then he chuckled. "An' there's probably no worse case of stubbornness in the world than a difference of opinion between a mule an' an Irishman!"

He looked across the fire over at Tom as he said, "I was surely glad enough when we reached Santa Fe. There, I bought a horse with the last of me saved-up railroad wages and rode West. And here I am."

"I'm sorry," Tom said. "Do you know the names of the men sent to kill you?"

"No. That's what makes it tough. They're Irish, is all I know. An' from me own village. So I hope at least I can recognize 'em before they can do me in. Francis Dillon had never spoken to them directly. He just heard village gossip, and then he heard it from MacDermot's own mouth."

Tom thought a minute, then he said, "Many men out here in the West have changed their names and started over. Reinvented themselves, so to speak. Have you considered that? If you change your name it might be harder for them to find you."

The Irishman shook his head no. He was silent as he thought about it, rubbing his chin absently with his left hand. Then he said, saying each word very slowly as if thinking out each word, "But that sounds like a good idea. I might consider doing that."

Peake sat quietly for an additional few minutes, looking into the dying fire, occasionally still rubbing his chin thoughtfully. He lowered his head and stared at the tiny red and yellow flames. Finally he looked up and across at Tom. "I have thought of the perfect new name for meself."

"What name is that?"

"Boyne," the Irishman said. "Jim . . . Boyne."

"Boyne?" Tom said, puzzled. It seemed an odd choice when a man could choose from any name he wanted.

"Boyne," the man said, "I think it a good choice under the circumstances. You see, the name Boyne translates to 'Foolish.' It will be my reminder, my punishment. For trusting that blackguard, MacDermot.

"Of course, under any name, I can never marry again. And I could never do that to an innocent, unsuspecting woman."

Quietly, Tom said, "I don't think you were foolish. I think you were remarkably restrained under the circumstances."

He thought of the many duels in Virginia's past, which were often sparked by a great deal less than what had been done to James Peake. For just the slightest personal insult, for example. Sometimes just an *implied* insult.

Suddenly Tom realized that the man's clothing fit so poorly because he probably hadn't eaten in a while. Who knew how long since Jim had eaten?

He thought of the cold beef and bacon he had, along with some biscuits. He got out the frying pan and put it on the fire, and shortly the Irishman was eating, gratefully.

As Peake was finishing eating, Peake's horse stamped and snorted, moving in closer to the fire as if to say, "Take care of me." So Tom said, "Has your horse had enough to eat today?"

The Irishman looked toward the dark at his picketed horse out there. "There was mighty little grass on today's journey."

Tom tossed his saddlebag to Peake. "There's oats in one side. Give your horse some. I have a nose bag in there for the horse to use to eat out of. Look in there, in the saddlebag. Do you know how to put the nose bag on a horse?"

"That I do. Thank you," Peake said. "Thank you kindly."

The Irishman left with the saddlebag and came back in a few minutes and sat down, handing the saddlebag back to Tom.

Tom was silent.

"What about yerself?" Peake asked.

"War troubles. After the last day of it, one of my brothers was shot and killed by a drunken Yankee, shooting his rifle at my brother out of a second-story window in an abandoned building below Richmond.

We were southwest of Petersburg. For no reason. Used my brother for target practice.

"The war was supposed to be over for us," he added bitterly. "The day before, we had been officially told to stop shooting. We were waiting to be told we could go home."

He could have said more.

Instead he said, "I came out here after that."

He thought for a bit, and then added something he had first learned after the war, in Texas: "A word of advice. Out here, it is bad manners to ask a man about his past. You size a man up, and judge him for what he is now."

"Are ye sayin' that a man might have something in his past or back East that he wants to hide from?"

"Maybe. Maybe not. Some have come out West to leave something—terrible memories of the war, or something that happened, or family troubles. . . ."

"Get a fresh start, are ye sayin'?"

"Yes."

"What about if it was something bad in their past? What about if it was a man like . . . a man as bad as MacDermot?"

"That, too. That's why you have to look a man over carefully, be careful until you get to know them—size them up."

"Ah, then, is that why you gave me the once-over when I came up to yer campfire?"

"Yes. That and I guess I wanted to be alone. Or at least, I thought I did."

Peake nodded his head in understanding.

"I'm findin' that it's more than a wee bit different

here. In Ireland, well, yer own people left, as you said, a hundred years ago, so let me explain.

"In Ireland, we have what my family has always called the Law of Hospitality. Anyone is welcome to what you have to offer, particularly if you're travelin' in an isolated area.

"Now, in England, in the rural areas, you might have to pay for a drink of water. But in Ireland, any stranger travelin' through a lonely area is welcome to water, as well as the warmth of yer fire and whatever might be in yer cookin' pot. It's a tradition so many centuries old, no one remembers where it started."

"Oddly enough," Tom said, "we have something similar out here. Ranch hands will usually welcome other cowboys passing through to coffee and whatever food there is at their campfire. And you offer a hand to anyone in real danger or distress, even if they might be your enemy in another situation."

"But ye size them up, whilst yer doin' it," the Irishman said.

"Now you've got the idea," Tom said. He felt oddly responsible for James Peake's welfare. He didn't know why.

"I may just as well tell you a few more things since you just arrived. It might just help you survive in Arizona Territory, 'specially in the desert areas.

"For example, always shake out your shoes or boots before you put them on in the morning."

Jim raised his eyebrows as if to question why.

"Scorpions," Tom said. "And spiders. Some spiders out here—their bite is poison."

Peake grimaced comically.

Tom continued. "Keep an eye out for snakes. I hear that you don't have snakes in Ireland. Especially watch out for ones that rattle. Their bite is deadly poison."

Jim Peake nodded as if he'd heard that before. He grimaced again at the mention of poisonous snakes. "True. No serpents in Ireland. What else?" he said, as if he might be afraid to hear. "I've already been warned about Apaches."

"I hear you have a lot of horses in Ireland, so I guess you already know not to wave to someone on a horse. Nod, so as not to scare the horse. You can slowly wave or signal to someone in the distance with your hat, if you have one."

Jim nodded that he knew that. "Only common sense."

"Out here, after you pass a man on a horse, never look back. It implies an insult, that you don't trust him."

"What if you *don't* trust him?"

Tom chuckled. "Then I guess you wouldn't pass him in the first place . . . unless you want a bullet in your back."

There were a few things he had learned on the Cooper ranch in Dallas County, Texas, that he didn't think Jim Peake needed warnings about, such as never bother or ride another man's horse, or never shoot an unarmed man, or never shoot women.

Jim had already indicated that he was not a violent man by his story.

In fact, now that he knew him better, Tom's impression was that James Peake was far more a scholarly, thinking man than a ruffian.

Not a man to rob or kill Tom while Tom was sleeping.

There was one more thing that Jim Peake might need to learn: caution. Especially since Peake had so readily approached Tom's fire and what with him being one who believed in the Irish Law of Hospitality.

So Tom continued: "Never wake up a Western man by touching or shaking him. He might shoot you. And Westerners don't like complainers or cowards. Neither do Indians. If you come upon Indians it is very important that you not act scared ... even if you are."

Jim Peake shook his head, his expression one of concerned concentration. Tom had a feeling that Peake would not forget what Tom was saying.

One other thing Tom had learned during his years in Texas, and needed recently traveling through New Mexico Territory and down below here in southern Arizona Territory.

"Sometimes your horse is all that stands between you and death—either from thirst, or Indians, or whatever. Always take care of your horse *before* you take care of yourself. Especially water and food. Well, I guess that's it," he added.

Whatever else Jim needed to know, he would learn by himself.

It was pretty much all that Tom himself knew so far.

Chapter Three

Suddenly, he was tired again. All the day's worries and fatigue returned. Tomorrow he'd be back facing all his own troubles—and his journey.

And it was enough talking for one night, and indeed, more talking than he'd done in a long time.

But he was pretty sure that he liked Jim Peake.

Jim got up and went and removed the nose bag from the horse out there in the darkness and brought it back to Tom. He sat back down where he had sat before as Tom stuffed the nose bag back into the saddlebag.

"I'm going to turn in now," Tom said. He picked up his blanket, shook it, and laid it back down on the dirt.

The fire, surrounded by a small circle of rocks, would go out by itself. In fact, it had already gone to half-inch-high flames as they talked.

The full moon was a brightly glowing circle of

ivory partway up the blue-black night sky. It would be a moonlit night.

Tom pulled his saddle up close to use as a pillow.

Jim got up and removed his horse's saddle and copied what Tom did, bringing his saddle to use as a pillow and the small saddle blanket for a bed. He stayed on the opposite side of the fire and lay down in the sandy dirt on the saddle blanket.

Tom gave him his saddle blanket to use as a top cover. Nights got chilly.

Jim watched as Tom took off his boots, put them to the side, then tucked his pant-leg bottoms into the tops of his socks.

"If it's all the same to you," Jim said, "I'll be sleepin' with my shoes on, after hearin' about the scorpions and spiders an' the like." He tucked his pant legs into the tops of his socks as he had seen Tom do.

In the quiet after that, both men fell asleep.

Jim was still snoring softly as Tom woke up at dawn. Tom sat up, put his boots on, restarted the fire, and began to make coffee.

As he used the butt of his rifle to crush some coffee beans, Jim woke up.

"Is there anything you want me to be doing?" he asked as he sat up.

"Not right now," Tom said. "I want to tell you one more thing. I don't know if you remember from last night, but I worked on a horse ranch in Texas a while back, and I kind of got the nickname Slim."

Jim stretched, yawned, and rubbed his left shoulder

where it was sore from sleeping on it. Then he looked at Tom in the gradually dawning light.

"Looks like it might be a good name for you," he said pleasantly, not implying in any way that he suspected any reason for Tom's name change.

Tom finished with the coffee beans and put the coffeepot on the fire. He took some bacon and some biscuits out of his saddlebag and gave Jim a biscuit to eat while he put the bacon in the frying pan.

It was quiet except for the distant early-morning chirping of small birds. Neither man had much to say.

After they were done eating, Jim followed Tom's lead when he saw Tom begin to cover up all signs that they had made a camp there. The fire remains were well covered with dirt, and everything was carefully cleaned up and put away. They watered and then fed the horses, and Jim returned the saddle blanket to Tom after shaking it out well.

Tom couldn't help noticing that Peake looked down and depressed this morning.

When everything was cleaned up and the horses saddled, Tom realized that he didn't know where Jim was headed.

Jim was riding what could only be described as an old nag. The brown horse had certainly seen better days, and Tom was well aware that a man was often judged by the horseflesh he rode out here.

He guessed it couldn't be helped for now.

"Which way are you going?" he asked Jim.

"Thought I'd go north, toward the copper mines," Jim said. "I've done a good bit of digging in my life; perhaps I can work in the mines up there. People said

Casey's Journey

to try the one called Buell's Mine. It's supposed to be northwest of here, near Buell's Crossroads. And yerself?"

"West."

A thought occurred to him, and he decided to say it to Peake. "Jim, right now, you might think your life is ruined, but if you're still waking up each morning, it isn't. You can start over—new—out here."

Tom looked around at the beauty of the land surrounding the two men. Red rock buttes jutted up in the distance to the east. It was hard to take your eyes off them, they were so beautiful. He didn't think he'd ever get tired of looking at the tall red rock spires and buttes.

Jim looked at them and solemnly nodded agreement. "It is beautiful country, all right."

Tom mounted Blacky.

"You might want to make yourself less conspicuous as a newcomer out here by buying yourself some new clothes."

Jim looked embarrassed. "As soon as I've two coins rubbing together in my pocket, I'll do just that."

Tom reached into his vest pocket and pulled out two double eagles. Each double eagle coin was worth twenty dollars. He leaned down and held them out toward Jim Peake.

"Consider this a loan toward your new start in life," Tom said. "I can spare it."

"I couldn't take those," Jim said, looking at the two coins as if Tom was handing him live snakes.

"Why not?"

"What if I never saw you again to pay you back?

And what if I stayed poor and never could pay it back?"

"Then we'll just consider it a gift," Tom said. "Here." He dropped the coins abruptly into Jim's hand, gently kneed Blacky, and rode off before Jim could consider giving them back.

As he approached the nearest junipers, he turned and said, "Good-bye, Jim . . . Boyne." Then he rode off out of sight.

"Good-bye, Slim Casey," Jim said.

And as he passed by the junipers and out of sight, Tom felt better and more hopeful than he had in a long time.

Chapter Four

Perhaps it was the breathtaking beauty of this land, or the wide panorama of sky. But this morning, something good had happened to the heavy weight he had carried in his heart for so long. It had lightened a bit.

Telling James Peake—no, Jim Boyne—that he had a new chance here had suddenly made him realize that maybe he, also, might have a new chance.

Although his troubles were still terrible, for the first time since the war, he felt a glimmer—the tiniest bit—of hope.

So far, General Brown's men hadn't found him, and maybe they'd stopped looking.

He knew he'd never give up looking for Angus Brown, Jr., though. The thought of that was always in his head.

Even if he could never go home, out here in the quiet beauty—the incredible beauty—maybe there was a place for him, as well as a place for Jim Boyne.

A place out here that, if he found it, he could call home.

A place of his own.

As soon as he finished this urgent errand, he would begin looking.

He wished Jim well.

He looked up. The sky somehow never seemed as big in Virginia as it did out here. Back there, smaller bits of blue sky showed through the tall treetops and along the roads. Fields were the places where the most sky could be seem, and yet it was so little compared to here out West.

Here, the sky often stretched right down to the horizon all around, broken only by canyons or mountains in the distance. It was as if there was a great, deep, clear blue endless dome over your head.

As he rode, he thought about the heavily forested state of Virginia. When fields were cleared for planting in Virginia in the spring, it was always a fight to keep the forests from creeping back in, taking over, and making the fields smaller.

Many different varieties of trees were lush and green and beautiful in Virginia. Virginia itself, of course, was beautiful, especially in the spring when the trees were in flower—but this out here, he thought, was a totally different kind of beauty.

It was a beauty dominated by large spaces and long, spectacular views. Spaces here were large. Inconceivably large, he thought. Spaces where a man from the East on a horse could say, "Can I really ride across all that distance?"

Casey's Journey 29

And it might take days to cross what land you were looking at from a rise or a high tableland.

Once, he'd talked with a man who said the buttes they were looking at in the distance were over one hundred twenty-five miles away.

He had crossed a lot of land, through the grasslands of the panhandle of Texas, then through New Mexico Territory. Now he was here in Arizona Territory.

He had ridden horses all the way here from Virginia.

His beautiful Virginia thoroughbred was not equipped for this rough land, so he had sold it early on to a Texas rancher and purchased the sturdy, Western-bred black gelding he now rode.

Home. He thought about his home in Virginia.

David, his oldest brother, had gone back home after the war to rebuild. So had his youngest brother, Will. Their one other brother, Ben, who was two years younger than Tom, was the one killed after the end of the war by the Yankee. He was twenty when he was killed.

It was a stupid, terrible waste of a very kind person. A terrible thing to do, and a bitter thing after Ben had survived the whole war.

During the fall of Richmond, they had fled, ending up southwest of Petersburg, fleeing from the advance riders of the Union cavalry.

And Ben's death—the shooting—had happened so fast.

They were camped near some trees close to an abandoned building that had once made inexpensive clocks.

Tom was sitting next to Ben when the shot came. One minute Ben was sitting there, leaning up against a pine tree, alive and joking with the men around him.

They were all happy at that moment, believing that they all would soon be going home.

The next minute Ben was shot in the chest.

After the first few seconds of shock and disbelief, Tom had grabbed his Spencer and run across the space and into the main doorway of the building and up the stairs. He rapidly searched the second floor of the clock factory to find the room that the shot came from.

He saw a man disappearing out a door at the far end of the large room, seconds after he entered. Tom had not had a glimpse of his face. And Tom was not a back-shooter. There was a small, dirty, unshaven middle-aged man in a blue uniform cowering in the far corner of the room, and the man quickly said, looking frightened to death, "It weren't me! It weren't me! It was that man there, Angus Brown!" he said as he pointed to the doorway that Tom had just seen the man run out.

To check out the man's story, Tom grabbed hold of the barrel of the rifle that the man held. Sure enough, the barrel was stone cold.

"Been out of ammunition for two days," the man said, almost crying, still cowering in the corner.

Tom believed him.

He ran to the other end of the room to chase the fleeing man, but not before he noticed two large empty whiskey bottles on the floor near the window that the shot had come from.

Tom had one thing in mind; to find and kill the

Casey's Journey

Yankee who had killed Ben. He wanted to shoot the Yankee in the chest. In exactly the same place he had shot Ben. His rage—a terrible rage—had obviously frightened Will.

Will had rushed into the upstairs room as Tom was leaving. Other friends and fellow soldiers—some who had known him since he was a child—poured into the room, also. Will had a look on his face of terrible shock and grief. Will was only eighteen. Barely fourteen when the war began.

In the instant before he left it, Tom saw the room was now filled with soldiers from Tom's outfit. They, too, were outraged at what the Yankee had done.

His best friend since he was a child, Red Duffield, appeared in the room and followed Tom as he raced down the stairs on the other side of the building.

Red, Ben, Will, and he had stuck together all during the war. His oldest brother, David, was not with them during the war.

Tom knew that among his fellow soldiers he had had a reputation for being cool and calculating and thinking things out, until this one day.

That day, in fact, was the last time he had seen Will or Red or any of his fellow soldiers.

He and Red had searched for the Yankee. All he had was the man's name.

By the fourth hour, he had information that Angus Brown knew someone was after him for the killing and had fled. It was near suppertime. Tom had sat by the fire, overwhelmed by grief and exhausted from his frantic search. A man in a Yankee uniform crept up to his side and whispered in a tense voice that he needed to talk to Tom.

Tom looked at the man and sized him up. Some instinct told Tom to take this man seriously,

Red and Will looked at Tom and said, "Don't go."

Tom said, "It's all right," and followed the soldier off, out of sight, behind some nearby pine trees.

The soldier spoke in a low voice. He said, "General Brown heard what happened. He heard you have vowed to get Angus, his only son. So General Brown has vowed, also, to get you. He say he doesn't care how long it takes. It's a personal thing, to protect his son's life.

"The general knows the truth about it, about what happened," the Yankee whispered. "He doesn't care. He heard that you are going to hunt down Angus. General Brown means it—he has sworn to get you. To stop you from killing his only son. If you want to escape General Brown's men, you better leave right now, tonight. I can't talk any longer. I have to leave. If General Brown knew—"

"Wait," Tom had said. "One more minute. What does Angus look like?"

"Medium height, brown eyes, sandy-blond hair, and a triangular-shaped face," the Yankee said. "I'm sorry he did what he did to your brother. Angus is evil. Gossip is that he'll go west, to East Texas. His family has relatives there." With that, the Yankee slipped away into the darkness.

Tom didn't know why the Yankee did him that favor, but he knew that he would never forget the Yankee's face. Some deep gut instinct told him to trust this Yankee, and he did.

He left right away, that night, riding west.

It was true. Tom had vowed out loud in front of everyone, kneeling in front of Ben's body when darkness was near and he hadn't been able to find Angus Brown, Jr. He vowed to find and kill Angus Brown, Jr. Because of Ben. Poor Ben. An honorable soul.

Ben had worn a succession of pairs of small gold-framed eyeglasses to see with since he was eleven years old. A kid who'd been picked on as a child, for his eyeglasses and for his small stature. Tom had always protected Ben, except for that day....

Ben had been a much better person, a much more sensitive human being, Tom thought, than he himself was. Than he had ever been. But that drunk Yankee didn't care.

Tom went west, to East Texas, with nothing but his pistol, rifle, and horse. Like many ex-soldiers of both sides.

A year or two had gone by, and he had not located Angus Brown, Jr. Always, everywhere he traveled he checked out anyone named Brown in Texas. And always he was looking for a triangular face.

He had not been successful. And always, anytime he heard men speaking with a Yankee accent, he had always been on his guard in case they were General Brown's men, sent to get him.

He'd never thought it safe to go home, what with the troubles in the South after the war and General Brown's vow to get him. He didn't want to bring more trouble to the plantation than it already had. Reconstruction and carpetbaggers, and the fire in his family's house, were enough for his family to worry about in the confusion and punishment of the South after the war.

In Texas he was only one of a great many men in similar situations, many who had fought on the side of the Confederacy.

Finally, he'd gone to work on a horse ranch in East Texas, where the men had just called him Slim. There were a lot of men without any apparent last names, or only vague first names, there on the horse ranch. Although he had been very skinny during the war, the horse ranch work had left him still slim but with a lot of muscle.

That first year he had grown to burst out of his shirts as his muscles in his upper arms grew. He had the broad-shouldered body of a man who did a lot of hard physical work.

He had not been unhappy on the horse ranch. He'd been accepted as one of the ranch hands, and had made friends.

And then the letter came a few weeks ago. That had changed everything again.

The news of where he was had been slow in reaching the big white mansion in Virginia—still pretty much in ruins from the war—and an answer was slow in returning, going first to an uncle in Kansas and then down to the horse ranch in Texas so General Brown wouldn't be able to locate him.

And so it was just recently that he had received the news about his youngest brother, Will.

Tom had left the horse ranch and headed west right after he had received the letter.

The letter was a long one, the longest letter he had ever received from David.

Dear Thomas,

I am sorry to have to write and tell you this but I am hoping that you can help. Something—well more than one thing—has happened.

Mother is very ill. The doctor says that she is dying. You must have heard from Uncle Clarence in Kansas that Poppa has died. It has been very hard here without you. After the war, I was sure you would come home and we could count on your help to rebuild. But that didn't happen, of course, as you well know. Well, maybe it couldn't be helped, although you might have acted differently, as I would have if the exact same events happened to me. I do tend to think before I act. You might want to consider thinking before you act in the future.

Anyway, that is not the reason for this letter. It has to do with our youngest brother, Will. There was some sort of ruckus between Poppa and William just before Poppa died. In fact, some of our family members feel that if the great squabble between Will and Poppa hadn't happened that Poppa wouldn't have had an attack of apoplexy and died on us the very next day.

The thing is, Will has run off—even further out West than you have. The argument was terrible. It was about Will's possibly having been a spy during the war for the North. I heard the rumor and told Poppa and he confronted Will and it was chaos. It was not my fault, of course, as I had no idea that the ensuing fight would end up such as it did.

Will has run away and is supposed to be heading for somewhere near Lame Horse Canyon, which is somewhere out in Arizona Territory. It is supposed to be in an area where there is red rock. That is all I know. Will's best friend Robert Morse told me where Will is headed on the condition that I relay this information to you only. You remember him; you were with him and Will during the war. Please find Will and see if he will come home. Mother is on her deathbed and wants to be reunited with Will before she dies. As you know, she is very willful and is cross with me as she blames me for the whole misunderstanding, and possibly Poppa's death. She is afraid that Will might harm himself.

If Will is not a spy, please see that he comes home if it is at all possible, as I feel that the circumstances are almost making me ill, also.

By the way, I heard that your old friend Ned Duffield, I think it is, runs a dry goods store in Santa Fe. If you contact him there, he could probably get a message back here sooner than Uncle Clarence could.

With Mother so ill and so willful, one has to wonder if she has in mind to remove me from my inheritance, which I hope will not happen as I do deserve quite a bit for all that I have done for her. I feel she will hang on long enough for Will to get home.

*Sincerely,
Your beloved brother,
David Casey*

What a pompous fool! My brother David hasn't changed a bit, Tom thought to himself.

That was one reason that he, Ben, and Will had joined the war together and David had gone his own way. The three youngest brothers had looked out for one another all during the war, and had grown very close. Poppa and David eventually had been assigned to gathering supplies for the Confederate Army. Poppa dead! And under these circumstances!

What had happened to his family?

He needed to find Will and find out what the spy business was all about. The thought that his youngest brother, Will, was a spy, was ridiculous! And suicidal?

Will would probably never forgive himself if Mother died and he didn't get back to see her in time. Will had never seemed to butt heads with her the way that he himself did.

There was no mention of Tom coming back in the letter; but of course, there wouldn't be.

But where was Will? Was he safe? What had happened to him to make him run away like that? He wasn't a person to run away—and he certainly wasn't a spy.

He was being blamed for Poppa's death—at least by David. Did he blame himself?

Tom knew that whatever had happened, it was not

Will's fault. He had spent the war years with Will. Will was a good person. Dependable. He always did what was right.

How could the rumor of Will's being a spy get started?

Tom knew one thing. He had to go and find Will and find out the truth. Whatever it was.

"Harm himself" was his mother's way of saying that Will might commit suicide.

Would Will do a thing like that?

Will had surely changed, as Tom himself had, since the war. Will was scarcely more than a kid—eighteen—when Tom had seen him last.

I know that, Tom said to himself. *We all have changed. But would Will go so far as to actually commit suicide? Did my going to Texas searching for Ben's killer instead of going home contribute to Will's troubles?*

He'd left Will to go home by himself. To deal with David, the pompous, self-righteous, greedy fool.

If he'd lived, Ben would be twenty-three now. He was the third of the four boys.

Will was twenty-one, and he'd always had Tom's protection when dealing with the war and with their own family: Mother, Poppa, and David. He was the youngest, and Tom had always felt responsible for Will.

And they'd lost Ben.

And then Tom had left Will, the baby brother, with only David, the pompous fool, to depend on back home.

Tom was wracked with guilt.

He had not only messed up his own life; but now it seemed that he had helped to mess up Will's, too.

Now Tom was heading for Lame Horse Canyon, Arizona. To try to find Will and make it up to him. And to find out what the heck was going on.

Will, a Yankee spy?

Chapter Five

P*oppa dead!* It was still hard to believe it. It should not have been that much a surprise, Tom thought as he rode.

He had known all his life that his father was a great deal older than his mother. She was twenty and he was forty when they married. Poppa would have been close to seventy when he died.

In some ways, it had not been a good match, even though his father had been a kind man. It was widely suspected by his father's family that his mother had married his father for one reason: money. She had married "up" and into more money than her family had, even though her family considered themselves old Virginia "aristocracy."

Her youth and beauty and the fact that his father had won her hand in marriage at all had affected the marriage in many ways. His father was so grateful to

Casey's Journey

have her that he had tended to let her be all-powerful and, truth be told, "the boss."

The truth was Poppa was afraid of displeasing her, and she had become a tyrant.

Tom sighed. It sure was getting hot. He took his hat off for a second and then wiped his face with his shirtsleeve. He put his hat back on. He thought some more as Blacky plodded on in the heat.

He hoped the Irishman was making out all right.

He saw a few mirages in the distance. Soon, he became lost in thought again, after he had taken a drink from his canteen.

It was not that his father wasn't a smart man. He was. And he was right about a great many things, even though he was told to shush by his wife when he tried to discuss certain things at meals that Mother considered boring, like business.

Her attitude toward Poppa and his meekness with dealing with what she had become had made the four sons lose a great deal of respect for their father.

Tom remembered vividly one day talking with Poppa in the enormous, opulent room Poppa used as his office.

It was in 1860, the year before the war started.

Poppa had showed Tom a map.

It was a current map of United States railroads. There was an article accompanying it, which Poppa read aloud to Tom, which said that railroads were now outranking canals.

The Midwest, the article said, had the most railroad tracks and the most trunk lines coming in to them. The main Western trade, the article said, was no longer North to South and visa versa, but more and more just back and forth West to East.

The South was being left out.

Where the railroads went, small towns grew into wealthy cities. The accompanying map showed this growth.

Where the railroads failed to go, cities and towns shrank and fell onto hard times.

Businessmen of the South, the article continued, had so far failed to comprehend the unbelievably vast potential of the railroad.

It cited the fact that in 1840 New Orleans had been the leading port city, but by 1850 both New York and Philadelphia surpassed New Orleans. The network of railroads in the Northeast and out to the West were flourishing, and the South was being left in the dirt, so to speak.

Because of easy access of traveling by railroad, the article stated, New Englanders were settling the Upper Midwest and bringing their antislavery ideas with them.

The name of the article was "A New Revolution in Progress: Bands of Steel Cross Upper America."

A small article off to the side said that John Deere, a Vermonter, had invented a plow in 1838 in Grand Detour, Illinois, that was unsurpassed in plowing the Midwest prairie soil.

Tom knew why Poppa brought this article to his attention. Poppa had been trying for years to get Mother to allow him to invest in railroads. She'd said no; it was a stupid idea.

This article showed that his father had been right.

Later, Tom saw the railroads help the North win the war. Supplies and troops traveled swiftly by railroad to where they were needed.

Tom was abruptly brought back from thinking about his parents by the black gelding's sudden alarm. The horse shied, went up on his back legs, and came down off to the side, almost sitting on his tail.

Tom had all he could do to hang on, until Blacky regained his footing.

He looked quickly around. What had spooked the horse? The horse was prancing nervously, and looking off to the left.

Finally, Tom saw the source of the horse's alarm as he and Blacky were passing a good-sized prickly pear cactus plant.

"Whoa, Blacky, be careful!" he gently chided the horse. "It's all right." He patted the horse on his neck.

Off to the left, near the cactus, there was a battle going on. A very large snake was trying to swallow a rattler. The rattler was fighting back, but losing, as his head appeared to be already somewhat down the other snake's throat.

Tom stared, fascinated, from a safe distance, so as not to spook Blacky. How did that snake have the courage to dare to eat a rattler? Wouldn't the poison kill that snake after he ate the rattler? He guessed not. That second snake seemed to know what it was doing.

He watched as the two snakes writhed in the pale yellow dirt. It was a silent battle except for the odd, but now weaker, buzzing of the rattles now and then.

Tom was silently cheering on the snake that was

eating the rattler. *One less rattler,* Tom thought. *Great!*

In a few minutes, satisfied that that was the end of that particular rattler, he moved on.

Blacky was still nervous. Maybe Blacky was right. He thought of what someone had told him once in Texas: if you see one rattlesnake, there is likely to be another one close by. He didn't know if that was really true.

Somehow he just had the idea that this desertlike area might be a very "snakey" area, and he was no great lover of snakes. As a kid, David had once thrown a garter snake at him.

As he looked up in passing, he saw a black, white, and red bird that looked like the same kind of woodpecker as there was in Virginia. It had a little red spot on the back of its head.

He rode on. He hoped that he'd make Lame Horse Canyon, wherever it was, by nightfall.

A few hours later, he saw a small but neatly built shack as he came over a rise.

He was not intending to stop, and in fact, had started to circle out around at a good distance from the shack so he would not have to yell "Hello the house"—or get shot at.

It was obviously a very small mining operation he had come upon, judging from what he saw.

As he rode, he saw that in fact the distance he circled around had put him in the center of an area of small foothills and rocks varying in size from pebbles to giant boulders, most of them red, some of them brownish-gray. Some of them had stripes of white and

Casey's Journey

cream color in them. Three of four large prickly pear cactus plants were close by the boulders.

A woman popped up behind him, cursing, from behind a small hill.

He was surprised.

He'd never heard a woman curse before. His mother, certainly, would never even have spoken to a woman who cursed.

She said the word again, loudly.

She was bending over, struggling to lift something in front of her in the dirt. It just looked like a fairly large ordinary rock to Tom. She wasn't succeeding in lifting it.

She tried again, still unsuccessfully.

She was talking out loud to herself.

She hadn't seen Tom yet, and she was talking to herself. "Men are useless. They are a pain! How did he expect me to lift this? What a fool!"

Blacky took a couple of steps toward her.

"Oh!" she said as she looked up, and then stood up straight. She had either heard Blacky's footsteps or maybe heard Tom make a noise; he wasn't sure if he had made one in his surprise.

The fairly tall, well-built, yellow-haired woman stood fifteen or twenty feet away from him. An old Colt in a well-worn brown leather holster looked right at home on her right hip. She stood for a moment, moving her arm the slightest bit as if deciding whether to remove the gun from the holster.

She didn't.

And she was the first woman he had ever seen with men's trousers on instead of a dress.

Her trousers were brown and matched in color the brown loose blouse she wore tucked into the waistband of her pants. She had on high brown leather boots almost up to her knees.

Not to mention a small flat-topped brown man's hat, keeping her head out of the sun, and secured under her chin by a chin strap. The hat was like ones he'd seen pictures of that California cowboys wore.

It was then that Tom glanced behind her and saw that there was an opening in a larger hill behind her. He saw a wooden framework around the opening. The mine.

Remembering her remark, he said, "Sometimes, in the past, I have felt that exact same way about women."

He was referring to his mother, although he felt no need to say so.

She looked him over.

"Get over here and help me," she said.

"No. I don't think so," he said politely.

"What?" she said.

It was her turn to be shocked.

She acted as if she had never heard a man say no to her before. He knew that he was supposed to be polite to women, but she was being very bossy—and that reminded him of his mother.

He'd long ago made up his mind to avoid women who were like his mother.

"I need help. You're standing there with all those big dang unused muscles. Aren't you going to get down off that horse and help me move this rock?"

"No."

Casey's Journey 47

"Why?"

"Get your husband to move it for you."

"Fool! I don't have one."

"You're not out here alone, are you?"

"Is that what you're trying to find out? If I'm alone? Are you a claim jumper? Or a robber?"

"You obviously don't think I am, or you probably would have gut-shot me on sight, right?"

"Right." She paused, thinking that over, then shook her head in puzzlement and disgust. Under her dusty brown hat, her yellow curls shook just a bit as she turned her head.

"So if you're not a bad man, why won't you help me? Was it because I cursed?"

"No."

"Is it because I wear trousers?"

"No."

"Why, then? Are you lazy? Just too lazy to get down off that horse?"

"No. It's just that I don't like bossy women."

"Bossy?"

"Yes."

"Me? Bossy?" She seemed honestly surprised.

"You. Bossy,"

"Why don't you like bossy? Saves time. Usually I just say to my father, 'Get over here and do this.' And he comes and does it. Never bothers *him* when I tell him what I need done."

She thought a moment, puzzled, and Tom had to admit she made a cute little face as she said, "Actually, my dad thinks it's funny when I'm bossy."

"I don't think bossy is funny."

In Virginia he never would have spoken like this—so bluntly—to a woman. His mother would have fainted dead away to hear him talk like this to a female guest or even an acquaintance. Probably so would his brothers, he thought, chuckling to himself. The men in his family had always been gentlemen where ladies were concerned.

"Wait till you meet my dad."

"I don't intend to stay long enough to see your dad," he said. "I'm in a hurry."

"So you're not going to help me move this rock," she said. The way she said it, he knew that she was not the least bit annoyed anymore that he was refusing.

He sensed a slight change in her attitude. It was a lot more respectful, as if he had passed some invisible test.

Dang!

He slid down from his horse.

"Perhaps I would if you rephrase your original demand into a less bossy sentence."

She knew she had won when she saw him step down off his horse, and her eyes suddenly twinkled, so she overdid it, and in an exaggerated Southern accent: "Oh, dear kind sir, could you, would you kindly help little bitty ol' me with this big ol' rock? Please, oh, please kind sir?"

He could take a joke.

With exaggerated courtesy, he swept his hat off and bowed to her.

"Of course, kind miss." He walked over the small rise so he could figure out what it was she was doing, and why she needed a heavy rock picked up.

Casey's Journey

He handed her his hat to hold and picked up the large rock she indicated and set it on the small wooden tablelike trough.

It was heavy. Heavier than it should have been for its size.

Now he saw what it was she was doing. Man's work.

She had a small sledgehammer and she was crushing rocks which must have been taken from the mine.

He looked carefully at the rock he had picked up for her. It was reddish-pink rock shot through with what looked like crumbly white quartz. He couldn't see any gold.

There were several other mining tools next to the trough. There was a pick and a few things that he didn't recognize.

"Is your father in the mine?" Tom asked.

"Yes," she said. "Do you want to go in and meet him?"

"No. I believe I'll be on my way."

"Where to?"

"Lame Horse Canyon."

"Lame Horse Canyon?"

"Yes."

"You have business there?"

"Yes. Do you always ask all these questions of strangers?"

"No," she said boldly. "Only the ones I think are . . ."

"Are what?"

"Never mind." She chuckled to herself, tossed her

head, and handed him back his hat. "Are you looking for a job, by any chance?"

"No."

"Go to Lame Horse Canyon, then. I'm sorry about before. I never meant to ruffle your feathers."

"Wait. Have you seen a man—a young man with dark brown hair and brown eyes who is medium sized?"

"Yes. Hundreds of them," she joked.

She decided to be nice. She put her hands on her hips. "Who is it you are looking for?"

"My brother. He is supposed to be near or in Lame Horse Canyon."

"What is his name?"

"Will. William Casey. I need to get a hold of him. Sickness in the family."

"Hmmm. I only know one hombre who might fit your description. Hired gun. Saw him once near Lame Horse Canyon. Been over near there about a month. But I think now he's out at the Zeigler mine."

She pointed west to a series of mountains in the distance. "Near Lost Padre Mountain over there. Works as a guard; escorts the wagons."

She took a good look at Tom, looking at his sandy-colored hair, and at his features and at his green eyes.

"He doesn't look like you at all."

Will didn't look like Tom. Will looked more like Poppa, hair so dark brown it was almost black. Brown eyes. Huskier.

And while people might describe Tom's face with his yellow hair and high cheekbones as rugged, they would easily describe Will's youthful appearance as handsome. These same people—friends and relatives—had told Tom many times that he favored his maternal grandfather.

Tom shook his head. "A hired gun? No. That couldn't be my brother."

"Must be another Will, then. Sorry. That Will is the only one I know. Know lots of Bills, but no other Wills."

Tom put his hat back on. She picked up the small sledgehammer. Using the sledgehammer, she pointed it a short distance to the right.

"Water over there. Help yourself. Horse is welcome to some, too."

"Thanks."

He led Blacky over to where she had indicated. There was a small stream which appeared in a low spot in the rocks. It was hidden from sight in a shallow hollow and he never would have known it was there if she hadn't pointed it out.

As he drank he could hear the sledgehammer hitting rock.

After they had drank and he had refilled his canteen, he looked over toward the woman, but she never looked up from her work.

He had seen no gold, but he assumed she knew what she was doing. He had seen quite a bit of green in surrounding rocks, and he wondered if that could be copper. He knew very little about mining. He would recognize gold if he saw it, but he would not recognize other valuable minerals if he saw them, or even if he rode right over them.

But it was something he would like to learn.

As he rode off over a twenty-foot rise, he heard the sledgehammer still hitting rock.

He chuckled to himself. Just when he thought he'd seen everything: a lady miner. And in a man's pants. Wearing a gun.

In a few short moments, the mine and the lady were out of sight.

Now that he thought about it, he had seen no horses back there, just a burro in a pole corral near the shack. The burro was standing in the shade of a small shrubby tree. Tom hadn't been close enough to see what kind of tree it was. Maybe cedar or juniper.

He fought with himself as he rode off. Should he go west? Should he keep riding directly toward Lame Horse Canyon, or seek out the man the lady miner had mentioned?

He kept trying to dismiss it, but there was still this feeling of doubt persisting.

Finally deciding, he turned Blacky off the trail and toward the direction the woman had indicated. Toward Lost Padre Mountain.

Chapter Six

At first Tom couldn't believe his ears because he first heard faint, then louder and louder singing.

The words to the song "Jimmy Crack Corn" became louder and louder and finally Tom knew that as he passed over the top of the next rise he would see who was singing.

As a precaution, he automatically loosened his rifle in its leather sheath, and his "Confederate Colt"—the Griswold and Grier revolver—in its holster, although he doubted that anyone announcing their presence this loudly was intent on bushwhacking him.

And not afraid of Indians or robbers, either.

Presently, he stopped Blacky and waited for the man to appear. The man was coming toward him from a trail that came up from the south.

His loud singing voice matched his appearance—somewhat flamboyant. Tom saw the largest man he had ever seen riding a much larger mustang than he had ever seen. The man had the largest, reddest beard—and Tom guessed probably the reddest head of hair under his large black hat—that Tom had ever seen.

The man stopped, a smile lighting up his face as he saw Tom.

"Ho, stranger! Good to see you on this fine day!"

Tom had to smile. Such jubilance he hadn't seen in a good long while—in fact since the beginning of the war.

"Ho!" Tom said. The man's good nature was contagious.

"Where are you heading?" the stranger asked.

"Up a ways, to the Zeigler mine," Tom said.

"Me, too!" the stranger said. "Bringing mail."

It was then that Tom noticed that sure enough, two large brown leather pouches hung from the man's saddle horn.

The man turned his horse slightly so that he and Tom rode close enough to talk.

They rode along in silence for thirty seconds and then the stranger spoke again in a friendly way.

"Aren't you afraid fer yer scalp?"

"Aren't you afraid for yours?" Tom answered back jokingly. "I would gather not, from the sounds of your singing." He added sincerely, "It's not that I didn't appreciate your singing... you have a very fine voice."

"Thank you," the man said, in a good-humored way. Like many men that Tom had met since working in Texas and traveling through New Mexico Territory, the red-bearded stranger was very soft-spoken.

Casey's Journey

At least when he wasn't singing at the top of his voice.

"The Apache Red Cloth is a friend of mine. He has sent the word out that I can carry the mail undisturbed. No brave would dare dispute Red Cloth's orders."

He chuckled again. Tom noticed that the man held the horse's reins like a man with a lot of experience. He rode tall and relaxed in the saddle.

"I guess that my red hair is additional protection. If one of his braves scalped me, Red Cloth'd recognize the scalp in a second and they'd be in trouble."

They rode on, the creak of the leather saddles the only noise for some time, along with the clop-clop of the horses' hooves in the dirt.

"My name's Ned Trumble."

"Slim Casey."

Trumble nodded. Then he continued in a friendly voice, "Today, I visited a friend of mine near here. Thought I'd bring this mail as a courtesy to the miners, so long as I was so close anyway. Otherwise, they wouldn't be getting it until next week when the regular man comes through here."

Chapter Seven

It was farther than Tom realized to the Zeigler mine area.

As he and Ned Trumble rode west, they came over the crest of a hill and before them stretched an enormous sweep of land. Perhaps it was a valley but he couldn't see either end in the distance. There wasn't much at all in the way of vegetation in sight. Not even desert plants.

In the far distance, at the other side of the great space in front of them, was a line of what looked like light gray-brown desolate-looking mountains.

One lone thin grayish-cream-colored dirt trail—really nothing but two wagon-wheel ruts—stretched before them in the dirt and off into the distance and eventually up into the mountains facing them. There was no sign of any vegetation on the mountains, either, at least from here.

Maybe up close . . .

But nothing else. Emptiness and distance.

He could sense rather than hear his companion chuckling at Tom's discomfiture. Then Trumble kneed his horse and started on down, ahead of Tom, into the great long stretch of area in front of them.

Although they looked close, Tom knew from experience in New Mexico Territory that the barren mountain slopes facing them were really very far away.

It seemed forever before the mountains seemed to get any closer as they traveled toward them.

By that time, Tom could see that in a deep fold of land just before the mountain, a small town—if that was what it was—was gradually appearing.

"Don't get yer hopes up," Trumble joked. "It's just five or six saloons. It ain't a real town, such as a Southern gentleman such as yerself might be used to. It's for the convenience, you might say, of the miners on the mountain up above. One evening," he continued, chuckling to himself, "some of the mining people—proud citizens, you might say—got tired of the saloon tents, gamblers, and what-not camped up near the mines and threw them all out.

"So they settled down here at the bottom of the mountain. Built these here buildings up ahead with their profits. Done quite well. Some say better than the miners do."

He chuckled again, and clucked at his horse, which had stopped while he was talking.

"If I may be so impolite as to mention a thing like this to such a fine gentleman as yerself . . ."

He looked to Tom for approval whether to continue

with his story and Tom nodded yes. He wanted to hear.

Still chuckling, Red continued, "One of the ladies married one of the gamblers and he named the town after her. So that there little group of buildings, that there town ahead of us, if you can call it that, is called Betty."

They rode closer to the mountains and to the small town.

Just before reaching the town, the trail swung around to the right so they came to the south end first.

They didn't stop for long in the town of Betty, but plodded on through, stopping only to water their horses at a watering trough placed in front of the aptly named Wagon Rut Saloon.

It was a thirty-foot-long building with a porch running along the front of the building. The porch had three chairs on it, and faced Lost Padre Mountain.

A few people waved or called out hellos to Ned Trumble, and Tom had the feeling that he was lucky to be somewhat under the protection of the big man. It was a rough-looking bunch, but Trumble, he could see, was respected here.

After watering their horses, the two men passed out of the town, still traveling parallel to the mountains just behind town. Eventually Tom could see the trail took a sharp turn to the left and began winding straight up and toward the mountains.

Three-quarters of the way up the mountain they were heading up into, he could see something above him on the smooth surface of the mountain which

Casey's Journey 59

made Tom think that that was where the mine was located.

Once again he was wrong.

The road, if you could call the wagon ruts a road, was misleading, because as it climbed, it went into a valley between two mountains, which developed into a canyonlike area.

Clinging to the steep right side of the canyon, it was dangerously narrow and made many switchbacks. Its twists and turns wound up and around, often disappearing from sight except for the small section directly in front of them.

It seemed like a very long time before, above them, he could see what he had thought was the mine again.

It wasn't.

What he had seen from down below clinging to the side of the mountain was not the mine at all, but a settlement. A settlement that was set far enough back on a small mountain bench, so that it was practically invisible from the bottom of the mountain, from the land they had first traveled across, and from Betty.

They passed one wagon road going off toward the canyon in a different direction. Tom let out a breath as he looked straight out.

The view from where he sat on Blacky was so large, so far, he couldn't really comprehend how far he was seeing. He couldn't comprehend that much distance.

And they were only three-quarters of the way up that mountain. Up close, the mountain's rocks looked different. They were gray and some were gray-green. He supposed that the green was ore—tarnished copper.

He had liked southern New Mexico Territory while passing through it, but this—this was something different. It was a place for rugged people, not the faint of heart, he thought.

Ned, sitting beside him on his own horse, had stopped to look when Tom did. Again, he was understanding, and amused. From Ned's attitude, Tom knew that he didn't need to speak. Ned seemed to understand what Tom was feeling.

Ned said, "Come on," and kneed his horse gently to urge him to go on up the trail.

Tom did the same, following along behind Trumble as he led the way.

From here he could see the mine farther up the slope. Below it, down here was the cluster of buildings and tents, perched on either side of the narrow road. Some of the buildings were perched on bits of land too narrow. Some backs of the buildings were held up by long poles, in effect hanging off the mountain.

The front of the buildings facing the street sat right on the edge of the road. Porches, if they were there at all, were all the sidewalk there was.

Tom wondered about the safety of those buildings on the side that dropped off so suddenly. They tended to be tall skinny buildings made of planks.

The road turned at the end of the settlement and curved abruptly around so that the next "street" was farther up the mountain lying parallel just in back of the first street.

It was a town literally hanging off the side of a steep mountain. With steep drop-offs.

"I suppose you'll want to eat at one of the restaurants on the inside part of the road?" Ned joked. He looked pointedly at one of the restaurants hanging on the edge and then at a restaurant across the street on the upper mountain side of the road, which was backed into the rocks of the mountain behind it.

"Guess you're right there," Tom said, only half-joking.

How could these people live in this dangerous place? He guessed they were used to it.

He saw people nonchalantly taking shortcuts down the mountain between the two streets by cutting down through the areas between the perched buildings to the lower street. Scrubby-looking grass and weeds grew in the spaces between the buildings.

He looked and saw that in some places there were steps and pathways between the buildings to go from the upper street down to the lower one.

Looking down past the lower level, he could see straight out—into nothing but space. He was not scared, but he was in awe. In awe that people would actually live up here.

"Come on," Ned said again, good-naturedly, and once again Tom followed as Ned rode farther upward on the road, which was still only two wagon ruts.

He guessed that his opinion about the safety of the buildings was right, as he saw the remains of a building that had already slid ten feet down the mountain, and was coming apart. People walked by, ignoring the abandoned building.

Before long, Tom and Ned came to a hitching post and Ned dismounted, tying his horse to the rail. He grabbed a bulging leather bag off his saddle and threw it over his shoulder.

Tom dismounted and tied Blacky. Ned handed the other leather bag to Tom.

The path from here on up to the mine looked anything but straight. Tom flung the leather bag over his shoulder as he had seen Ned do, and they started up the increasingly steep trail.

"There's eight or ten miles of mine dug right underneath us here where we're walking," Ned said.

Tom was not happy about visualizing that under his feet right now. Was a mess of mine shafts crisscrossing underneath him? What if they caved in?

Ned seemed to be enjoying Tom's unease. He chuckled.

They walked for at least five minutes. Once they had to step aside as a wagonload of ore went by, pulled by mules. Tom noticed that the mule skinner had to constantly keep the brakes on so that the wagon didn't overrun the mules.

Tom also noticed that the road was carefully graded to make it as level as possible for the mules, using switchbacks to go down the mountain instead of straight downward paths.

Going down, then, was not so bad as he would have thought for the mules, and coming back up, the wagons would be empty.

"Where is the ore going, Ned?" Tom asked.

"You can't see it from here, but there are big rock crushers, called stampers, down the mountain a ways, in one of the canyons we passed on the way up. You can't see them from the road."

Casey's Journey 63

The stampers must be on the road, then, that went off toward the canyon. "Oh," Tom said.

"Would you want them big ol' crushers going up here, vibratin', shakin' everything to kingdom come?"

"No, no, thanks, Ned. I see your point," Tom said. "That's the *last* thing I'd want to see," he added, making a comical face.

Ned laughed, and then turned and continued on up.

Then, miraculously, there it was. The mine opening. A small but well-built building stood near it. The building was about twenty-five feet away from the mine opening. It wasn't perched, but sat on a place that had been dug out and made into a large, flat area on the mountain.

The flat space was large enough for at least ten mule teams and wagons to occupy and turn around safely. As it was late in the day, the space was empty now.

A man came out of the building. He looked like the man who was in authority. He called out "Trumble, you old ranny! What you been up to?"

As he said this, he swiftly walked over and reached for the leather bag Trumble had been carrying.

Tom knew from his Texas days that the man was complimenting Trumble. Ranny was short for ranahan, which meant a real good, efficient cowboy. A good worker—it implied a good person.

"An' who's this skinny pirate you got with you? He one of them quartz-reefers?"

Ned turned and translated. "He wants to know if you are a prospector lookin' for gold."

"No," Tom said, grinning at the man.

" 'Zat mail, too?" the man said, pointing to the bag over Tom's shoulder.

"Yup," Ned said.

"Gimme that, then," the man said. "You carried that long enough. That lazy Trumble give that to you to haul up here?" the man said, obviously joking.

Tom handed the mailbag to him.

"Yup. Gimme the lightest one, though," Tom said.

"That I doubt," the man said. He pretended to weigh each one by holding each one out and bouncing it a bit.

"Nah," he said. "Ned's is about a pound lighter." He chuckled and said, "Come on inside."

He turned and headed toward the building and Tom and Ned followed him.

Inside the building, which appeared to be mainly an office, was a single, neatly made up bunk on the left and a small metal cooking stove on the far back right.

Two lit oil lamps hung from nails hammered into the ceiling beams, one near the desk and one near the stove. The glass sections of the oil lamps were almost black; they hadn't been cleaned in a long while.

The room smelled like yesterday's fried onions, which Tom could see were still in a frying pan on the stove. Next to it was a blackened metal coffeepot.

Tom saw a tablelike desk on the left, covered with a lot of messy piles of papers. There was no other table.

Wood shelves along the walls held an assortment of cooking implements, food supplies, and other things such as shaving items.

Casey's Journey

There were two chairs made of pine in front of the desk and one behind it.

The man hurriedly put the mail pouches on the bunk, and went to the stove and brought back the coffeepot, which he put on a metal trivet on the desk. He had to push aside papers to put it there. Then he went and got three cups off a shelf near the stove.

He motioned for Tom and Ned to sit.

"Sugar is in that small pot there," he said in a friendly way as he began pouring the coffee.

He indicated Tom as he spoke to Ned. "This one raised on sour milk, or prunes, or proverbs?"

Ned chuckled, "He's askin' if you are grouchy, too particular about things, or overly religious."

Ned chuckled again and said, "He don't want a job here, Alwin. You don't need to interview him."

He added, "In fact, from the expressions on his face on the high and narrow parts of the trail, I think he'll put some speed on gettin' his tail back down off this mountain purty dang fast.

"He ain't here for a job, no sir. He's just here ahuntin' his long-lost brother. Alwin Jones, I'd like you to meet Slim Casey."

There was a slight, almost imperceptible shift in Alwin Jones's demeanor. Gone was the jolly man happy to see Ned and his friend.

It was now that the man paused to really look Tom over. He did not like what he saw. He stiffened.

Tom knew that Ned noticed it, also.

Ned was blunt. "What's the matter, Alwin?"

"You say Casey?"

Tom nodded.

Alwin reached down and took the welcoming coffee cup out of Tom's reach.

"You'd better leave," Alwin said. "Now."

Chapter Eight

"What! Why?" Ned said. Tom could see that he was trying to come to Tom's aid and defense. But it was also clear that Ned thought highly of Alwin and didn't want to anger him or lose his goodwill.

"Never you mind. Just leave. Now."

Ned looked dubiously at the two men.

"Well, I guess you'd better leave, then," Ned said. He put his own coffee cup down.

Alwin stood, and watched as Tom left the small building.

Outside, Tom said to himself, *Now what in tarnation was that all about?*

Ned stayed inside, and Tom had the feeling that he would question Alwin and find out what was going on.

Tom was puzzled, because the Will he knew—had grown up with—was a man whom Alwin would have liked, Tom was sure.

What the heck was going on here? Alwin Jones had acted as if Tom had the black plague or something.

Tom went down the trail from the mine until he was out of sight around a sharp corner, then found a rock and waited. It was sunset.

He hadn't eaten since breakfast, he realized. He sure could have used that coffee.

That welcoming coffee had been jerked away on short notice.

He couldn't, didn't, want to believe that Will had done something that bad. Something so bad that Alwin had reacted to the name Casey like that.

Never even asked for a first name. Never heard the name Will. Just Casey. Casey had been the word that had brought the change to Alwin Jones's face. He was Casey's brother. That was enough to get Tom thrown out of there. Pronto.

Casey. *Watchful,* the Irishman had said last night. Watchful, not evil. Not so bad a name that a man's brother needed to be thrown out.

What was going on?

It was fifteen or twenty minutes before Tom finally could make out the form of Ned Trumble coming toward him in the dusk. The sun had set directly behind the mountain they were on. It would be completely dark shortly.

Tom was embarrassed to face Ned after what had happened. He was glad it was dusk and Ned couldn't see his face. The thing was, he couldn't see Ned's face either. He had no way of knowing what was going on with Ned. Was Ned angry at him? Did he blame Tom for what had happened?

Casey's Journey 69

In the waning daylight, Tom could see by his profile that Ned had the empty mailbags over his shoulder.

In a way, Ned could think that Tom had used him to get to see Alwin Jones. But that wasn't true; although Tom alone knew that. At least Ned didn't tell Tom to get away from him.

Ned seemed to be aware that Tom had arisen from the rock where he was sitting waiting, and was following him back down the mountain toward their horses and the buildings that sat down the mountain from the mines.

They reached their horses and the small glow from the buildings below them gave them enough light to reach the restaurant that Ned had mentioned before.

As they pulled up in front of the restaurant, Ned said shortly, "You'd better wait out here. I'll bring us out something."

Ned tied his horse to the hitching post and went inside the restaurant. He didn't bother to ask Tom either for money or what he wanted to eat.

Tom was worried even more. It was *that* bad? He was in danger if he was so much as *seen* in a restaurant here?

He dismounted, and holding the lead instead of tying Blacky to the hitching post, he sat on a nearby rock.

Discouraged, he put his head in his cupped hands.

All the hope that he had felt after talking to Jim Peake—Boyne—was gone.

His stomach felt sick.

Will. What has happened to you? To us? To our family?

Shortly, Ned came out with a package.

Without speaking, Ned untied his horse and mounted.

Tom did the same. Obviously, they were leaving town before they ate.

Before whatever it was became common knowledge.

Tom hoped that whatever it was, he had not put Ned's next visit here in jeopardy. Was Ned in danger because of him? Because he had brought Will Casey's brother Tom—Slim—Casey here?

It appeared so. Ned did not stop to speak.

Or was this mine somehow tied to Gen. Angus Brown and Angus Brown, Jr.? That didn't seem at all possible. Was it *Slim* that Alwin Jones despised?

Worried, Tom followed Ned as Ned rode back down through the settlement. Ned offered no explanation. He was silent as the two men's horses passed along the bottom road of the settlement and on to where the lone, dangerous road led down the mountain.

Surely, Ned was not planning on making that trip down in the dark?

It had been a harrowing trip up, in the daylight. Tom couldn't imagine anyone foolhardy enough to chance the dangerous trip on the narrow winding wagon road at night.

Worse, if Ned went, Tom would have to follow. He would not want Ned to think him a coward, on top of all the rest of what had happened in the last hour.

He was relieved, then, when Ned pulled off the road

onto an area he obviously knew well. It was almost pitch-dark now.

"Here, this is wide enough for us to bed down. You roll much during your sleep?" Ned joked grimly.

"Not tonight," Tom said.

"There's about fifteen feet here of ledge here, if I remember correctly. Should be enough for us and the horses if we're careful."

"Were you intending to stay the night in the settlement?" Tom asked.

"Yep," Ned said regretfully. A touch of humor was back in Ned's voice, Tom was glad to hear.

"A couple of glasses of whiskey had my name written on them," Ned joked.

Tom was embarrassed to ask—but he had to.

"Did you find out anything? What did Alwin say after I left? What was the matter?"

The humor was gone and there was a sad bleakness in Ned's voice in the dark as he spoke. Tom also sensed that Ned had some sense of sorrow for Tom for what he had to say.

"It seems that your brother broke one of the most serious codes of the West. He did something unforgivable, as far as most Western men are concerned."

"What did he do?" Tom couldn't imagine what it was that Will had done that was so bad.

Ned was standing near Tom, and his quiet voice broke the silent darkness as he said bluntly, "Alwin said that your brother Will is accused of murder. Of cold-bloodedly shooting down two women."

Chapter Nine

"Will was in charge of guarding the assets of the mine," Ned's deep masculine voice near him in the dark continued, "and a man named Frenchie Malebolge—I dunno if I'm pronouncin' that right, comes from a strange family—anyway, this Malebolge was supposed to be smugglin' gold out of the mine."

"I thought that the mine was a copper mine," Tom said quietly, in the dark.

"Well, not exactly. You see, the Zeigler mine has four metals all jumbled together: copper, that's the most, but lead, and silver, and even some veins of gold mixed with quartz in it.

"Anyway, as you can imagine, men have tried all sorts of ways of smuggling gold out, in their pant cuffs, in false teeth, and who knows what else. But Frenchie was suspected of wearing a belt buckle with a secret compartment. Seems somebody saw him open the secret compartment and sneak some gold nuggets in there.

"Will was sent out to Frenchie's place a couple of days ago. Frenchie lived with his three maiden sisters, and when Will didn't come back to work—an' neither did Frenchie—day before yesterday a bunch of miners went out to Frenchie's place. It's only a half hour's ride from here.

"Anyways, when the men got there, two sisters were dead—shot, and with bullets from a .36-caliber revolver.

"An' no sign of the other sister or of Frenchie.

"Everyone knew what kind of a gun Will had. In fact, as you probably know, he had a gun exactly like the one you are wearing.

"That's what spooked Alwin so fast—him noticin' you wearin' the same *exact* copy of the revolver that Will had."

"We got them during the war. There were only thirty-five hundred of them made, I think," Tom said regretfully. He, Ben, and Will all had bought and paid for their revolvers with their own money.

"Those the ones made in Georgia?" Ned asked. "The ones supposed to be a copy of the .36 navy Colt?"

"Yes," Tom said.

"I had a Leech and Rigdon handgun from Georgia once," Ned said. "Fine weapon. Also a .36 caliber. Yankee took it from me," he added regretfully.

Tom heard a long sigh in the darkness.

Tom felt something touch his shoulder, and he realized that it was Ned, handing him a bare chunk of cooked antelope haunch. No plate, no napkin, nothing; just a chunk of meat.

Tom took it gratefully, began to rip off chunks of it with his teeth, and chewed.

It would have been funny, if circumstances weren't so dire, and worrisome. The irony of sitting in the dark ripping off chunks of meat with his teeth and chewing it like a wilderness animal, instead of at a lace-covered dining table, full of pieces of highly polished silverware and fancy china and crystal, as he had been so carefully raised to do.

And being dang glad to have it. Tasted delicious, with a few slugs of water from his canteen from time to time.

In a few minutes Ned passed him a chunk of bread. Tom ate that as well.

A few pinpoints of light—stars—began appearing in the immense, intensely blue-black sky above them.

Normally he took care of his horse before he ate, but tonight things hadn't worked out that way.

Feeling around in the dark, he was able to put the nose bag on Blacky and then on Ned's horse.

"What are we going to do about water for our horses?" Tom said.

"I saw a battered ol' bucket up the road a bit near one of the watering troughs. Outside one of the buildings," Ned said. "I'm thinkin' on borrowin' it later for a few minutes so we can water the horses. Can fill it at the trough up there."

"Good idea," Tom said. "Need any help?"

"No. One can sneak better than two," Ned said,

Casey's Journey 75

ironic humor in his voice. " 'Sides, I can feel my way around better than you," he said. "Know my way around the place. You, you might just go off the edge up there somewheres."

Their talk gradually stopped. An hour or so later, Ned said, "Sit here. Don't move. I'll be back in a few minutes."

He didn't have to say that twice.

Tom sat.

Ned was as good as his word. He was back soon.

Swiftly, they watered the horses and then as furtively as he had gotten it, Ned returned the bucket to where the owner had left it.

He made one more furtive trip and came back with the canteens refilled. Tom didn't ask any questions. He hoped, though, that the water wasn't out of one of the horse-watering troughs up there in the settlement.

He had enough faith in Ned that he believed that the water came from a clean source.

The moon rose and it didn't help. It only made Tom more aware of the narrow space they were on. The horses were picketed in closest to the mountain, on the inside, and Tom and Ned were on the outside, nearest the drop-off.

Evidently all movement up and down the mountain stopped at night.

"What makes it look bad for your brother is the fact that Frenchie was a knife man. He didn't even own a gun. He was deadly enough with his knife. One of them long daggers. Nobody would mess much with Frenchie. They knew that if they did, they might get a dagger in the back some night whilst they were sleepin'," Ned said.

"I can't... I still can't believe that Will would do such a thing," Tom said. "He was raised to be such a gentleman."

And it was Tom himself who had rebelled against his mother's obsessive, rigid rules of polite society, not Will. Will had seemed to like things the way they were back then.

"I'm going to make what might seem to be an odd suggestion, given the facts. But what I'm gonna say is this. I think you need to go over to Lame Horse Canyon an' have a talk with a gentleman named Texas Harper. He's a star-toter."

"A lawman?"

"Yes. He's about all the law there is around here. Covers the whole Lame Horse Canyon area. Town marshal. Dang good lawman, an' smart as a whip. Always beats my pants off at chess. Anyway, if anyone can straighten this thing out, it would be Texas."

"Texas. That's an odd name."

"Not if you know him. Big man. Used to be a Texas Ranger, when he was still almost a kid, an' wet behind the ears," Red said. "Was in the Mexican War."

Tom thought he heard a yawn.

"That's enough jawin' for one night," Ned said. "I'm turnin' in. An' I guess I can sleep, because I have a feelin' that you ain't gonna do much sleepin' tonight. We better plan on bein' shut of here come sunup."

He was right.

Tom spread his bedroll out and crawled in, but he couldn't sleep.

He just prayed that nothing spooked the horses in the night.

Nothing did.

At the first light of dawn both men were up and heading down the mountain.

Blacky seemed none the worse for wear from spending the night on a narrow ledge, and seemed eager and unafraid to make the trip down off the mountain. It must be his mustang blood, Tom thought.

A few hours later, he and Ned were back at the place where they had met. They hadn't talked much; each doing their own thinking.

"Head east, back the way you came, and take the first turnoff in the trail heading left. That will take you to Lame Horse Canyon."

"Lame Horse is a funny name for a canyon," Tom said. "Lame horses usually get put down."

Ned chuckled. "Not this Lame Horse. This Lame Horse isn't a horse at all. It's the name of an old Pueblo Indian who used to live up in that canyon. He had a bad leg. He's long gone now, but looked to be a hundred years old when he passed away a few years ago. Limped as long as I knew him. Some said it was a snakebite, some said it was a fall off a cliff."

Tom didn't know what to say. Ned had been a big help. He owed him a lot.

"What are you gonna do, after you settle this thing with your brother? You gonna head back to Texas?"

Tom looked around.

Without having to do much thinking, Tom was surprised at himself that he had an answer for Ned.

"No. Think I might stick around for a while."

Ned smiled. "Good. Hope to see you again, Casey. You seem to be a decent jasper."

With that, Ned touched his hand politely to his hat brim and kneeing his horse, rode off.

Chapter Ten

Now what made him say a thing like that? Until he'd actually said it, Tom assumed, himself, that he would head back to Texas.

Maybe his heart was quicker to comprehend things than his head was.

This country was a lot harsher-looking than East Texas. A land of extremes. High mountains, plateaus, and deep canyons. Beautiful.

Desert and forest. Desert plants, then junipers spotting the landscape, then tall pine forests. Or vice versa, depending on whether you were going up or down in elevation.

Now he was heading back toward red rock country. Red rock country was unlike anything he'd ever seen. More desert than not. Scrubby trees and bushes. Certainly not as desolate as near the mine.

The yellow rock he'd seen as he was crossing Texas was pretty, there was no doubt about that. Sometimes in the yellow rock in Texas he'd seen broken circles of balls of clear crystal imbedded in the yellow rock. He'd even put a small one, about the size of a small peach, in his saddlebag as a keepsake.

But this deep red and red-orange rock . . .

Blacky seemed to like this country, too. No doubt partly because he had been living a life of luxury lately, living on oats out of a nose bag rather than having to graze on Texas or New Mexico grasslands.

A land of extremes. Arizona only became a territory in 1863. Yet it had been settled for centuries, he knew, by Indians and Mexicans. He'd heard that there were very old ruins of ancient settlements in some of the canyons.

And he knew from talk back in Texas that during the War Between the States the Apaches had free run of Arizona because men were off fighting the war, leaving the settlers largely unprotected.

Ironically, he'd passed through Apache territory down south to the east of Tucson and had never even seen one.

From the view off the high mountain slope back there at the Zeigler mine, and even now, there was no indication that there was a canyon in the red rock buttes ahead.

Facing Tom was a wall of high red rock buttes and cliffs with no indication of any opening. No bunch of telltale trees indicating water, no apparent break in the cliffs. He couldn't see any visible canyon.

He had only Ned's word for it, and the faint trail he was on.

He traveled on.

Casey's Journey

Finally he came to what seemed to be the transition area between the barren, desertlike, harsh conditions of the southern part of Arizona Territory and this area, which was more hospitable.

Water was not a problem here, at least during this time of the year. Afternoon thunderstorms rolled in, dropped water, and rolled away quickly, and the sun came out again. Whitey had told him that, also. Whitey had lived up here a few years ago. The thunderstorms also served to cool things down.

The red rocks were now on each side of him and he began to see occasional cottonwoods and even some other kinds of trees—some that looked like a kind of oak—as he rounded a bend in the trail.

He had entered a valley in a deep canyon.

It was clearly a valley, although the ground was rugged and sloping here and there in front of him. The right side of the canyon was impassable, it was so steep. Possibly a man might be able to climb and walk there, but only on foot.

Riding on the wagon rut trail, he came to an area where the trail ran along a ledge area high on the left side of the canyon.

Below him to the right, he could see, not water yet, but tall, stately-looking cottonwoods which, from past experience, led him to know that there was at least a creek below him under the cottonwoods, if not a river.

It was too steep here for a horse, and maybe even for a man to climb down and reach the water below.

The trail went down again, much closer to the creek.

He passed a giant sycamore, with its spotted bark

on the creek side. It must be hundreds of years old. He passed a pasture.

Riding on, along the ledge, he saw below him, in a hollow where the downward slope of the ledge to his right ended, a building nestled among the cottonwoods.

Down below him, on the side facing up slope toward him, he saw that this side had been cleared of cottonwoods, but there was a large pole corral made from a type of rough-grained short logs of a kind of wood that he had never seen used before for that purpose.

Could it be cedar?

There was a side door from the large barn leading to the corral, so the horses could be let directly out of the barn into the corral. That was a good idea. Horses were in the corral, swishing their tails to keep flies away.

The trail gradually went down. It felt twenty degrees cooler in this canyon with the shade of the cottonwood trees than it did out in the direct bright sunlight that he had been riding through all morning.

It was a kind of paradise. And where this ranch was, and how it was built, indicated to Tom that Indians in this particular canyon, whatever kind they were, were not unfriendly.

The corral would never have been built backed up to a slope that Indians could slide down and get to the horses so easily.

On both sides of the canyon, which looked quite wide here, beautiful red rocks jutted hundreds of feet above him on both sides.

Casey's Journey 83

He noticed a little henhouse not too far from the barn, under some more cottonwoods.

A bee landed on a large white flower similar to his mother's blue-and-white morning glories, only larger, growing beside the trail. This white flower was on a rough-looking plant, though, not a vine, like the morning glories.

A little bit farther on he came to another house. This one was down below the trail, also. Down close to the creek bed, but high enough up the slope of the creek bed to be safe during flood times, Tom noticed.

Two homes, ranches really, out in this desolate area so far from anything? And was one of them Frenchie's?

Tom doubted whether this area had ever been even explored much. Maybe that was not true these days, since prospectors had been all over Arizona Territory for at least fifteen, maybe almost twenty years. Except for the war years.

He guessed it was not so unlikely to find two homesteaders here, especially since it was so beautiful, and had the all-important thing in Arizona Territory—water.

Because there was a town marshal, there must be more homes up the canyon, and a town. He dismounted and looked for a place to go down and reach the water. He and Blacky were thirsty. The water promised to be cool.

Finding a spot, he carefully led Blacky down the first slope. In a minute, he was under the cooling shade of the cottonwoods.

Ahhh. He closed his eyes for a second to savor the

coolness under the trees. Then he and Blacky walked down the next slope, and came to the flat area which Tom could see extended out on both sides of the river. It was an area that had obviously been leveled by the countless times the river had flooded and spread out over its banks.

There was one more descent of about ten feet, where he and Blacky had to be careful, going down at an angle, and then they reached the edge of the creek.

The creek was about ten or twelve feet wide, and flowing strongly. There were a great many rocks and pebbles of all sizes, even boulders here and there, and Tom kept a sharp watch out for snakes.

The river was flowing briskly and was sparklingly clear. After he had drank and replenished his two canteens, he bent over to inspect the small rocks in the cold water, which was only about six inches deep.

Black, white, and yellow butterflies flitted about on the other side of the creek. What looked like small white moths were also flitting around.

There were rocks of many different colors; green, gray, pink, red, and other colors shining in the shallow water.

On one small, black, bumpy-looking pebble he saw tiny, tiny specks of what looked like gold. The specks were so small he was not sure they were even there. It was not the silver-gold color of fool's gold, but was quite yellow.

He slipped the pebble into his pocket. The gold, if it was that, was so small as to be unusable, but it was still fun finding it.

Casey's Journey

I've got to stop loading myself and Blacky down with rocks, he said to himself, *even if they are small.* But he did not throw the pebble away.

A large gray boulder on the other side of the creek made him stop and think.

If the sides of the canyon on both sides of him, hundreds of feet high, were red, with just a bit of yellow or white here and there in various layers, why were the rocks in the creek bottom such different colors?

There were a few bits of red stone here and there, which looked like small bits of rounded red brick, but the vast majority were of these different colors.

After enjoying the water and the shade for a few moments, Tom realized that he'd better be on his way. He led Blacky up out of the creek area and back up onto the trail.

A mile or two farther into the canyon Tom came to what must be, he guessed, the town of Lame Horse.

It was very small. He passed Burton's General Store, Lucky's Saloon, Brady's Saloon, and came to a rock building that Tom guessed must be the jail.

A burly blond man, with a ball and chain on, was outside the jailhouse, cutting wood. There was no one else around.

Tom had never seen anything like that before.

The man saw Tom and grinned when he saw the expression on Tom's face. The man looked down at the ball and chain attached to his leg. "I ain't goin' nowheres, leastwise, in no hurry, with this on. Weighs about twenty-four pounds. Have to carry it when I move about. Too heavy to drag. You lookin' fer Texas?"

Tom nodded.

"Marshal's gone up the road a mite. Be back in three shakes of a lamb's tail." The man pointed to the hitching post and then to a bench in front of the jail. "Set a spell."

Tom politely touched his hat and dismounted. "Thanks."

He was a little surprised to see a prisoner outside the jail, chopping wood with an axe, and volunteering helpful information cheerfully.

The man knew what Tom was thinking, and said, "I only get ornery when I'm drunk. Was drinkin' some nasty bug juice at the saloon last night, over there, an' punched a pompous prospector what needed it. Texas had business up the road a ways early this mornin', so he left me to chop this here wood as punishment."

Tom took it that "bug juice" was whiskey. Maybe locally made. He sat, and a few minutes later a man who Tom took to be Texas rode into sight from the opposite direction that Tom had just come from.

He nodded politely to Tom and then proceeded to talk to the prisoner as he dismounted. He bent over and unlocked the metal rings around the prisoner's ankle attached to the ball and chain as he talked.

"Went out to the Warners' to see about the horse what was stole from the oldest son, Bob. All the while I was there the second from the oldest son, Little Albert, he's hangin' aroun' and lookin' like he was near to cryin'.

"Finally, after hearin' Bob's story about how the

horse turned up missin', I took one more look at how nervous Little Albert was still actin', an' I played my hunch.

"I looked at Little Albert and said, 'This horse what disappeared, it weren't never stolen at all, was it, Albert?'

"Whereupon, Little Albert commenced to cry. Two white lines of unusually clean skin runnin' from his eyes clear down to his jaws and then drippin' off onto the ground.

"I says, Albert, what I say happened is that you borrowed your brother's horse without permission an' took it for a ride. Is that right?"

"Well, Little Albert nods his head yes, whilst cryin' his head off and says, ' 'Tweren't my fault. Horse stepped into a badger hole and broke his leg. Had to shoot him. Never meant for it to happen, I swear.' "

The ex-prisoner said, "So the Warner horse wasn't never stole at all?"

"Naw. It was a family thing after that, so I come on back here." For the first time, Texas looked over and scrutinized Tom.

"Say, stranger, what can I do for you?"

Tom stood up.

The ex-prisoner showed no sign of leaving. Tom wasn't sure whether he should say much in front of him.

Texas was not what Tom expected at all. He was about fifty and had a rather large potbelly underneath his dusty, rumpled, completely black outfit which included a black vest with a star pinned on it over his heart.

He waited patiently for Tom's reply.

After a few seconds Texas caught on to the fact that Tom was unsure of whether to speak in front of the ex-prisoner, but waving that aside with his hand to reassure Tom, he said, "Come on inside. Jake, you skedaddle on home."

Jake said, "Yup," and leaned the axe neatly against the woodpile off to the right of the door of the jail. Then he walked off toward one of the small saloons.

Inside, the marshal motioned for Tom to take a seat. "That was just Jake Jameson," Texas said, dismissing further discussion of the man with a wave of his hand.

Sitting on one of the oak chairs in the plainly furnished room with one jail cell in the back, Tom told his story. He left out the part about the letter from home and only saying that he was looking for his brother who was supposed to be in the Lame Horse Canyon area. He told how he had been directed to the Zeigler mine; he told him what had happened there, and that Ned had said that Tom ought to talk to Texas.

He told how Alwin had acted at the mine and how his brother Will was accused of killing two women. He told how he didn't believe it.

The marshal nodded a few times as if he had heard parts of this story already.

At the end Tom added how Frenchie was thought to be robbing the mine of gold using a false-front belt buckle.

Texas rubbed the stubble on his chin. It seemed to be a habit that he had.

"Well, I can tell you some things about Frenchie that not too many people know," Texas said. "First of all, the three women are not his sisters. And he's not French.

"Truth is, Frenchie's parents were from Scotland. Frenchie did spend a coupla years in Paris when he was a youth, though.

"He and his two brothers used to be robbers. Worked along the Ohio River. Dangerous area. I had family from that area, so I know. Ol' Abe Lincoln himself was attacked in that area 'round about 1828. Was takin' a flatboat down to New Orleans. He escaped, but had a scar near his ear the rest of his life.

"That was before Frenchie's time. Anyways, Frenchie's last name is really Abermarle. First name Rowan. Rowan Abermarle. His two brothers were the main invited guests at 'necktie socials' for their part in a lot of robberies on the Ohio River. Suspects in a few murders, I'm afraid. Wouldn't be surprised at all if that were true. A rough bunch, that family."

A "necktie social"? They were hanged?

"Frenchie came West with his own wife, and the wives of his two brothers. The two women are widows of his two hanged brothers. They certainly *ain't* his sisters.

"Frenchie was trying to go straight, so I was pretty much leaving him alone. He was workin' in the mine. But I guess it was too much temptation for old Frenchie, workin' near all that gold.

"I guess I should have suspected as much. Shouldn't have given him the benefit of the doubt, so to speak.

"Anyway, the other thing is that all the three women weren't right, somehow, in the head. Probably weren't *never* quite right; marryin' murderers like they did, in the first place.

"Lived alone out there near the Lost Padre. Never had much company, but you can see why. Odd people. Odd family. There's not too many people hereabouts, and what people that there are, they stayed away from Frenchie's place.

"Three harsh women. Had tough lives for all that.

"Did you know I was out there day before yesterday, to Frenchie's? Miners came and got me. Couldn't figger it out. The door wide open and with the heat and wild animals . . . I almost got sick. Couldn't tell who was who.

"Do you know who was left alive? Which one of the three women? Was it Leslie?"

Tom shook his head. "I don't know."

"Leslie was Frenchie's wife. If it was her left alive, I'd suspect that Frenchie got tired of supporting his two widow women . . . or something else happened. If it was one of the other women Frenchie took off with, I don't know."

He thought some more.

"There could be a lot of explanations, that only included your brother accidentally, or because he showed up at the wrong time. Have to wait and see."

At least he wasn't outright saying that Will was guilty. Tom felt that here, no matter how odd Texas might look as a lawman, was someone who would try to find out the truth.

Chapter Eleven

"You got any explanation or any idea where your brother might have got to?" Texas asked.

"No. He was sent to Frenchie's is all I know."

"Doesn't look good, on the surface, the .36 caliber bullets . . ." Texas said.

"I know," Tom said soberly.

"You have that much faith in your brother? That he didn't murder no one?"

Tom was put on the spot. Then he said, "Yes." And he knew in his heart he was right.

At least he hoped so.

"As much as any human being can know another, I believe Will wouldn't murder anyone . . . especially women."

He felt he had to add something. "Of course, we fought during the war. . . ."

Texas waved him off.

"Among other things, I was in the war with Mexico.

91

Texas Ranger before that. Was a Texas Ranger in the '40s. During a war, it's war. That don't mean nothin'."

Again, Tom was grateful for Texas's attitude. It made him feel better about himself. It was something that had been bothering him ever since the war . . . had he been on the right side? It was one of those things that on a dark sleepless night, Tom went over and over in his mind.

So far, he had never found an answer that ended it, once and for all. Shooting at people he didn't even know. Had he been wrong in being loyal to his family and to the state of Virginia, no matter what he felt about slavery?

Texas seemed not to notice that Tom was lost in thought, because he himself was thinking, also.

"Well, mister, what do you want to do next?" Texas finally asked.

"I'm not sure," Tom said. "You think it will do any good to take a ride out to where the murders occurred and see if we can spot anything?"

"Like what? I already been there. Miners already buried the two women."

"Well, I thought we could check and see whose clothes are missing. Maybe know who is left alive that way. Only trouble is, I don't know the women and couldn't tell whose clothes are whose anyway. Is there anyone around who might know?"

Texas rubbed the stubble on his chin. It was obvious that he hadn't shaved in a few days.

"Well, I meant to go in and shave this off, but what you mean to do might solve a piece of the puzzle."

Casey's Journey

He squinted, and then said, "Know one lady who might be helpful. Nobody much was welcome at Frenchie's place. Jaspers out there kept to themselves, as I said, which was just as well. Anyhow, one time one of the women, Cora, was took sick, an' an old woman named Jolie Fenton nursed her back to health.

"Bein' an old lady, I guess Frenchie figgered that she couldn't harm them none if they was friends, so he let her on the place once in a while.

"Come inside while I make some bacon and eggs. You're welcome to some."

"Thanks."

Texas talked as he cooked. "We'll have to go get the old lady and take her to Frenchie's. That's a bit of a journey. Might take a little while."

After they ate, Tom waited outside, and it was fifteen minutes before Texas emerged. He had shaved, washed up, and changed clothes. His clothes were still black, but they looked clean and less wrinkled.

Jolie's house, which turned out to be the first of the two houses Tom had passed on the way into the canyon, was built of whitish-yellow rock, and had a low roof.

Texas Harper explained what was going on, and Jolie and her husband agreed to follow Tom and Texas, who led the way to Frenchie's place.

To reach Frenchie's place, the group rode back out of the canyon. Frenchie's home was on a turnoff, close to the town of Betty. It was a little-used turnoff which he hadn't particularly noticed before, running south along the mountain below Betty.

Frenchie's place was about what Tom expected

from what Ned had described. Made of rough unpainted planks, the small house, which looked more like a shed than a house, was untidy inside. Broken items, left unrepaired, littered the yard near the house. It apparently had been left as it was, when the murders were discovered.

The bodies had been removed and buried out in back of the house. Two rock-covered mounds were all that showed of what remained of the two women. Tom could see them as he looked out the small back window of the house.

Mice had already been taking advantage of the empty cabin. Even some larger animals were probably starting to enter through the loosely fitting door.

Jolie, a thin woman with white hair pulled back into a neat bun, with a blue-and-yellow calico dress on, shook her head in dismay.

"Things are in such disarray," she said, discouraged.

It was true. Clothing was scattered about. The plank table was overturned, as were some crude pine chairs. Dirty dishes littered the floor, some broken.

"We'll make three piles," Jolie said, stepping carefully over the mess. "One for Anna, one for Cora, and one for Leslie."

When it was done, it was obvious that only Anna's clothing was missing.

"What it looks like," Jolie said grimly, "is that Frenchie and Anna run off. Leslie's clothes appear to be all here—leastwise, what I know of them."

"Anna was the smallest, wasn't she?" Texas asked. "And the youngest."

"And the prettiest," Jolie added regretfully. "Cora,

bless her departed soul, was not a handsome woman. Had a three-inch knife scar on her left cheek from a fracas with her husband before he was hanged. But after a couple of days in this heat..."

That was why the bodies of the women had been so hard to identify, he guessed. And although they were discussing various heights and weights of the women, it was relatively small differences, he figured, by the way people were acting and talking.

Tom had already noticed that Cora appeared to be the largest of the three women from the clothing pile belonging to Cora. The dresses were for a large woman. Unless she just liked her clothing loose and baggy.

Anna's clothing, what few items had been overlooked in the rush, probably, to depart, were full of ruffles and doodads and such. Very feminine things.

Leslie's and Cora's things were more functional, utilitarian things.

Texas looked at the piles. Tom guessed that he had surmised the same things as he and Jolie were thinking.

"Still doesn't prove who shot who," Texas said, looking Tom directly in the eye. "Only shows that the two survivors—if they did survive and are not out there somewhere..." He nodded to indicate the desert. He clearly thought they might be dead.

"I know," Tom said.

Tom knew what else Texas was thinking—that if Frenchie wanted to get rid of Cora and his wife, Leslie, he would have used his knife. He could have buried the two bodies out away from the house and none would be the wiser. And then rode off with Anna.

No one would ever know the two women were missing. It would just be assumed that they all moved away as a group.

"You sure Frenchie didn't own a gun? To shoot game, and rattlers and such?" Tom asked.

Both Jolie and Texas shook their heads no.

But Jolie's husband wasn't so sure. He was a small man, with shoulder-length, pure-white hair.

"Thought I heard a gun go off near here once when I was passin' by, in the distance. Thought it came from here."

"One of the women might have owned a gun," Texas said.

It did leave an opening. Maybe Anna—

"What about a trail?" Tom asked suddenly. "What kinds of trails were there, leaving here?"

"By the time everybody and their cousins came to look at the bodies; too many. There were hoofprints all over the place, coming and going, by the time I got here," Texas said.

Tom looked around. It did look like there had been a fight or some kind of a tussle that took place in this room. But between whom? Will and Frenchie? Frenchie and Anna, against Leslie and Cora? Who?

Was Will out there in the desert, dead?

He looked around, but when he walked around the house, he couldn't see anything in the messy rooms and dilapidated kitchen that gave an indication of who it was who had done the fighting—or the killing.

Was Will shot here, too?

Chapter Twelve

There was every reason to believe that Will might have been killed.

Frenchie had made a living robbing and perhaps knifing travelers on the Ohio River. There was no reason to believe he'd have any qualms about killing Will.

"Anybody got any ideas of what else we can look for?" Texas said. "That idea to look for the clothing was a clever one."

No one answered.

The only thing that Tom could think of was to try to track whoever it was who had left the cabin. Even if it meant tracking every set of horse hoofprints in the area.

He said that.

The three nodded.

"You need help doing that?" Jolie's husband asked.

"No. Just be adding more tracks for me to worry about."

Texas looked intently at Tom, and seemed to be deciding something, by the look on his face. Finally, he nodded.

"You find anything, you just come get me. Personally, I think you'll be wastin' yer time, but I know it's a thing you feel you gotta do. Me, I think I'll go an' have a parlay with the folks at the mine. See if there was any ill will between Frenchie and Will."

"Thank you for your help," Tom said to Jolie and her husband.

He watched as Jolie and her husband rode off.

Texas said, "Think I'll stick around for a while and see if there's anything else I missed first time around. Kind of embarrassin', you comin' up with somethin' I missed." He smiled regretfully. "If you can think of anything else we missed here, I'd be grateful."

Tom nodded. "I'll think on it some as I ride."

Texas walked back inside the house and Tom rode off.

Texas was right, there were a lot of tracks all around the cabin.

Tom realized that he had one thing going for him, and that was that he had spent the last few years on a horse ranch. While he wasn't one-tenth as good as a trained tracker, he could at least figure out a few things that had happened.

First, he had to figure out if the three people leaving—Will, hopefully alive, and Frenchie and Anna—were on horseback, or were Anna and Frenchie or any combination in a wagon?

Eliminating wagon tracks that simply came and then left circling in the front of the house as sightseers, he looked first at odd wagon tracks.

He circled the house, following the odd tracks until he had satisfied himself that the wagon tracks all led back toward the mine, Betty and Lame Horse Canyon.

As he circled, he saw that in a dip in the land, there was a small hidden seep with water. Not good-quality water, either. You'd have to strain it through a cloth to use it.

A poor source, but one that at least allowed Frenchie and family to live here. Otherwise, it was a desolate spot most people would not have chosen.

Gritting his teeth in disgust, he filled his canteens, using his tin cup and his bandanna to strain the water into his canteen. *Ugh!*

But then, Frenchie had his reasons for wanting to be isolated, Tom guessed.

Past the seep, there was no reason to keep circling. Most of the tracks were back nearer the house.

He looked back at the house sitting out in the middle of nowhere, as he went back to tracking.

Eventually he eliminated the wagon tracks.

They were probably on horseback, then.

And he assumed that people running away, having committed murder, would not head back to where people would know them, toward Betty, or the Zeigler mine.

He concentrated on tracks, then, that led away from the seep in other directions.

Eventually, he came upon tracks heading east. One

set of tracks looked particularly hopeful. There were three horses in this set.

By the time he found this set, he was too far from the house to call out, but he looked back.

He took off his hat and used it to wave to Texas, who was standing, watching him from near the back of the house.

Texas took off his own hat and waved to Tom.

Soon Tom was out of sight of the house, by himself, in a desolate area, without even any shrubs.

Just tracks going off in the distance, in front of him.

He'd take a chance that these were the right tracks, but he could be wrong, dead wrong.

Or dead, if he were right.

It was very hot.

Three hours later, he saw buttes in the distance. The tracks headed straight toward an area, once again, that gave no indication that there might be a canyon.

It began to get dark. He made camp for the night, cared for Blacky, and was glad to crawl into his blankets. Although he thought some before he went to sleep, he didn't come up with anything else to look for in Frenchie's house that might be useful.

The next morning, he awoke at dawn, and was off again. It was very hot again, riding out in the sun. There wasn't a tree anywhere, and sweat ran down the sides of his face. He wiped it off with his bandanna.

After a couple of hours, he pulled some jerky from his saddlebag and chewed it along with a few sips of water from his canteen.

He arrived at the canyon entrance. Once again it was one of those hidden canyons.

Casey's Journey 101

This canyon was different, however. It was spectacular. The creek running along the bottom had a bottom of solid red rock. The creek was wider and more forceful than the gentler one in Lame Horse Canyon. It looked as if it came from a larger water source. It flowed west, out of the canyon.

And although at first the rock walls on both sides of the canyon were red, shortly the rock walls were out of sight and Tom was in a cool paradise of pine trees.

It was twenty degrees cooler in here, shaded by the magnificent pine trees that looked to be hundreds of years old. They grew on both sides of the wagon rut trail, and up the canyon slopes.

Here, the trail ran within sight of the bubbling river.

The trees had long, straight trunks without branches until near the top, and so Tom could clearly see the river and into the woods beyond on both sides, except where fir trees, with their branches down to the ground, blocked the view.

The tall pine trees had cinnamon-colored bark, with an orange tinge.

Tom led Blacky down and they both drank from the clear, cool creek water.

Tom emptied out his canteens and filled them with the creek water.

He mounted up, and continued on the trail.

It was silent except for the gentle noise of the running creek water.

In his mind, he named this Paradise Canyon. He could picture living here. Pine trees could be cut down for logs to build a cabin. The canyon was wide enough to plant crops back from the creek.

As Tom rode further, the red rock of the creek, polished smooth by the water that had evidently flowed over it for centuries, gradually turned, like in the Lame Horse Canyon, into rocks of all different colors.

Was this a box canyon? What was at the end of it? Was he riding into a trap?

He kept a sharp lookout, but he kept riding. Every once in a while, in a hole in the tall trees above him on both sides, he would get a glimpse of red rock high up.

Further in, the red rock disappeared and he saw only trees on both sides of him up the high canyon sides as he rode. Trees as high up as he could see. This canyon was very, very deep.

He saw that the trail didn't just end at the back of the canyon. It began to make a series of bends and began making a lot of switchbacks and heading upward.

The switchbacks went along the side of the wall at the end of the canyon and then back, zigzagging so that instead of being steep, even wagons could make it up the curving trail.

The trail used every bit of cleverness to climb upward using the easiest path available. This must be an ancient Indian trail, he thought. He felt a silent appreciation of the man or men who had either designed or discovered this trail.

At one point, where he was on a ledge and there was nothing between him and a drop-off, he got down off Blacky and walked as near to the edge as he dared.

He couldn't believe how high up he had come. The tall trees blocking his view before this had hidden just how steep the canyon walls were below him, and how high up he had come.

Even here, he could only see giant, slim-branched pine trees all around him. Even below.

The giant dark-green points of many of the tall pines—they must be one hundred or two hundred feet tall—were all around as he looked out into the deep canyon bottom he had just left.

He knew he would never forget the surprise, the beauty of this moment, as long as he lived.

Nearer the top, he realized that he was coming out on a plateau. Tom decided that this would be a good place to stop and give Blacky a much-needed rest.

He pulled off the trail a few hundred yards, out of sight. It was pleasantly shady under the pines.

He made sure Blacky was taken care of and picketed before he unrolled his blanket on the brown pine needles under the trees.

Pulling another piece of the dreaded but necessary jerky out of his saddlebag next to him, he wryly thought to himself that Slim was an appropriate name.

His stomach growled and kept him awake for a while but exhaustion overcame him and he was soon asleep.

Late in the afternoon, he awoke.

Mounting up, he rode over what appeared to be the crest at the top of the canyon and found himself in a beautiful flat area of forest with the same kind of pines that grew down below.

Although down below, other kinds of trees grew

near the creek, up here on the plateau, the forest was made up of the huge pines.

The pine forest was clear of undergrowth. Pine needles were beneath the trees. There was a slight breeze. The smell of the pines was wonderful. He couldn't believe he had found this beautiful, peaceful place. He had left the heat behind in the desert. The temperature here was pleasant.

As he rode, way up ahead of him, he saw a skunk leisurely cross the trail. He slowed Blacky down, giving the skunk plenty of time to get across the trail before he and Blacky reached the point where the skunk had been.

The skunk was gone by the time Blacky crossed his path.

After a couple of miles, the trail headed downward, and after the trail made a couple of abrupt turns, Tom could see a settlement in the distance.

Behind the settlement, to the north, stood three or four giant dark-looking mountains of black-gray rock, covered sparsely with timber on the lower levels.

The wagon rut trail he was following widened as other trails joined it, and it began to look like a path that was used frequently.

It was a good guess that there were sawmills near. The pine trees, which appeared free for the taking, must be worth a fortune, he thought.

Chapter Thirteen

Following the wagon tracks, Tom noticed that Blacky's ears quivered just the tiniest bit, and turned forward to catch every sound. There was a slight rise just ahead, blocking Tom from seeing what was ahead.

He chuckled, saying to himself that if he had someone to bet with, he'd have bet a golden eagle—twenty bucks—that there was a woman ahead.

The reason for the bet was that Blacky liked women. He'd been raised by a woman.

There were some men that Blacky didn't like, and in fact, it had taken a while for Blacky to come to trust and like Tom, but Blacky had a soft spot where women were concerned. Blacky's ears were cupped straight ahead, so he could catch every sound.

He snorted to clean the dust out of his nostrils, so he could sense the woman better. Tom chuckled.

He would have won the bet.

As he came over the rise, he saw that in a spot

where there was a steep downward drop in the trail, a wagon had overturned at the bottom of the slope.

There was a brown-haired woman about his age. Near her was the overturned wagon.

She looked as if she had been crying, but she turned away and used a portion of her pale yellow dress to wipe her tears before she turned around to see who was approaching. Her dress had a white collar and cuffs, with an ornate lace panel down the front. The dress had a bow in the back, and accentuated her small waist.

Straightening her back up, she turned to face Tom.

From her untanned face, Tom guessed that she was a newcomer out here. And he guessed she was an Easterner, judging from the delicate material her dress was made of.

She had a dirt smudge on her left cheek, and there was a small tear in her dress, now that he looked more carefully.

She took a deep breath, closed her mouth, and waited for Tom to speak first.

He looked and saw that she was alone, and the wagon was empty. She was frightened by his arrival and what had happened. She had a pretty, kind-looking face.

"Are you hurt?" he asked.

"No. But the wheel is . . ."

She moved out of the way, and he looked.

The left front wagon wheel had three broken spokes.

"I can fix that for you," Tom said, swinging down off Blacky and smiling at the woman to reassure her.

Casey's Journey

"Thank you," the woman said gratefully, breathing out the air she had been holding inside, and moving out of his way.

Luckily, the chunky, white-spotted mare pulling the wagon did not seem injured. Tom straightened out the harness.

He went over and put his back under the wagon. He used his back as a wedge. He managed to flip it back over.

As he flipped it, he realized the wagon was built too light in the first place for this rough terrain. *Bounce around too much, on these rough roads,* he thought to himself.

He could tell by the look on the woman's face that she was surprised at how strong he was.

He suspected that her inexperience had caused her to come over the rise much too fast, and that ruts, stones, and bumps had caused the wagon to flip.

She knew that he knew that the accident was her fault. He could tell that by the way she was looking at him.

"I can get this fixed good enough to get you home," Tom said, looking at the damage. "But you'll need a new wheel."

She nodded. "I can't pay you," she said too quickly. She was trying to make him believe she had no money on her.

He thought for a moment, and then decided that the truth was important here if this well-dressed woman was to survive long traveling alone. There were rough men here, and very few women.

"Wrong thing to say," he said gently. "First of all,

if I were a robber—which I'm not—what you just said would make me suspicious that you *did* have money on you—and quite a lot, from how worried you're actin'. A person who has little or no money on them doesn't fear being robbed.

"An' second, most men where I come from would be insulted and their feelings hurt if you suggested paying for just doing the decent thing, and helping a stranded person out. 'Specially a woman. Just a thank you will do."

Purposely ignoring her so that she would not be afraid, he politely kept his distance and didn't glance over at her as he went to his saddlebag. He took out a piece of rawhide, and began cutting it into narrow strips with his knife.

Using the strips to tightly bind each broken wagon wheel spoke back together, it only took him about ten minutes before he had secured the three spokes well enough to get the wheel back in working order.

"Take it easy, and that'll get you where you're going safe," he said.

He put the rest of the rawhide back into his saddlebag and put his knife away.

"Thank you," the woman said. She climbed back up and sat on the wagon seat.

He knew from the worried look on her face that he was right; she *was* carrying money.

Because she wasn't carrying any leather bag or pouch, he guessed that it was probably in a pocket in her yellow dress.

"Thank you, Mr. . . ."

"Casey. Slim Casey," Tom said.

"I'm June Webster. I used to be a schoolteacher back in New Hampshire. And you are right. I am carrying money. Money very precious to us.

"My brother Harry and I are building a house over on Lame Horse Creek and I'm on my way to the lumber mill up ahead to order lumber. My brother's been feeling poorly, so the job of ordering lumber fell to me.

"If you'll permit me, I'd like to quote Thomas Paine to you: 'Virtue and intelligence are not hereditary.' In your case, I don't know where you got them, but you appear to have both these wonderful qualities, virtue and intelligence. And a nice way of caring about other people. Good day to you, Mr. Casey."

He tipped his hat to her, and she picked up the reins, clucked softly to the horse, and drove off slowly without looking back.

She was spunky, he had to give her that. He guessed she would make out fine here, once she got the hang of it. She had come all the way from Lame Horse Canyon, and up the steep canyon trail he had just climbed.

In fact, she might have passed by as he was sleeping.

He watched until she turned off the trail up ahead, her wagon turning left onto a side road into the trees.

He thought that that must be the road to the sawmill. He'd have to remember that.

He continued on his journey toward the settlement ahead.

Chapter Fourteen

Tom rode up to the buildings in the settlement. it was larger than the town in Lame Horse Canyon. There were the usual saloons, jail, banks, and other buildings. Most were made of wooden planks. A wooden sidewalk ran along the front of the buildings.

A saloon which had a sign hand-painted in large white letters on the front of the building announcing GOOD WHISKEY seemed as good a place to start as any.

He tied Blacky up to the hitching post in front and went inside.

Walking up to the bar, he said, "Whiskey," to the bartender, a man with a round face, black hair parted straight up the middle, and a black, full mustache parted in the middle as well.

The ends of the moustache dropped off the man's chin on both sides of his mouth a good inch or two, making him look somewhat comical.

Casey's Journey

"Comin' right up," the bartender said good-naturedly.

When the bartender placed the glass of whiskey in front of Tom, Tom paid him, and then picked up his drink. He walked over to a table and chose a seat with his back to the wall, facing out.

He pretended to be drinking, but he was really listening.

There was a mixture of people in the saloon. U.S. Army soldiers, miners, cattlemen, farmers, and a few rough-looking men who looked like cattle rustlers.

Three men over in the far left corner were talking. They looked like cowboys from Texas, rather than California. They wore high-heeled boots, big hats, shirts, and overalls.

"You can catch them wild horses up in the canyon by riding them down," one lean cowboy with shoulder-length yellow hair was saying. "I learnt that by watching the Indians. Work in relays. Change mounts. Have hosses stashed in a few places beforehand. You gotta haze them hosses into corrals you already got built at the end of the canyon. Then you keep the best horses, and let the others go."

"Nah," the second cowboy said. "You wait at a water hole, build a corral, then stay away a coupla days till the smell of you goes away. Then you come back and drive them into the corral." The second cowboy was a lot older and had a lot of wrinkles around his eyes. Probably caused by years of squinting in the bright sunlight. He looked like he knew what he was talking about.

The third cowboy said nothing much until they were discussing the length of stirrups. Then he said, "I like to see two inches of daylight 'tween a man an' his saddle when he stands up in the stirrups. That's how I adjust 'em."

Tom silently agreed with the third cowboy, although he said nothing.

The talk gradually drifted to something else: "Doc Cory says she was beat up real bad. Teeth knocked out an' everything. These two teeth," the first cowboy said, pointing to his own two crooked front teeth.

"Not gonna look so great anymore," the second cowboy said.

"What makes a man do something like that?" the third man said.

"She said—she told the Doc that he was charming one day, beat her the next. Wanted his own way all the time. A complainer, she said. Complained all the time about other people's imperfections, as if he was perfect himself. Only did all this when he was drunk.

"But the strangest part was that she was ranting and raving about her and Frenchie still having a prisoner tied up outside of town somewheres. Doc didn't know whether to believe her—she's mighty addled in the head by the beatin' she took. Talking mighty loco."

Frenchie!

So as not to seem conspicuous, Tom sat there and finished the rest of his drink. Leisurely, he got up and returned the empty glass to the bartender, nodded to the bartender in a friendly way to indicate that the drink was fine, and left the saloon.

He passed a group of people just up the street in

Casey's Journey

front of a general store. They were standing on the wooden plank sidewalk talking. He heard bits of gossip which indicated that the Frenchie-Anna fight was the current topic of gossip in the town.

He got the impression that Frenchie and Anna and the other two women were not unknown in this town. In fact, they seemed to have lived here for a time before moving near the mining area down below.

He continued on down the street, listening to whatever gossip he could, until he spotted a sign that said DOCTOR SETH CORY, *specialist in Lung Ailments and Broken Bones.*

The doctor's office was upstairs on the second floor above Murphy's General Store.

At the top of the stairs, Tom knocked.

"Come in," a deep male voice said.

Tom went in.

"What can I do for you?" the doctor said. He was a smallish older man wearing a wrinkled gray suit with a vest, and small eyeglasses perched on his small nose. A gold watch on a chain hung on his vest. There was no pistol in sight. He held a wet white cloth with blood on it in his hands.

Tom wasn't sure just what to say. Finally he decided to just plunge ahead. "Do you have an Anna Malebolge here?"

The doctor gave it away by glancing toward a curtained-off back room. "Why?"

"I have reason to believe she is involved in two murders," Tom said.

The doctor's eyebrows went up in surprise. "You sure of that?"

Tom nodded yes. "You know where Frenchie Malebolge is?"

"That I do. I believe he is in the hoosegow—the jail—about three doors down from here."

"How is she doing?"

"Okay." Then he reconsidered, and whispered, "Actually, not good. I think her insides are smashed up," the doctor said in a whisper.

He paused and then added, "I was surprised that Frenchie only *hit* her . . . he's known for using a knife. Townspeople here in Pine Vista are surprised at that. So am I. It's not like Frenchie.

"He's a man with a short fuse, especially when he's been drinking. But he seemed stone-cold sober when I saw him being taken to jail. That in itself was unusual."

"Don't let Anna out of your sight," Tom said. "She might be a dangerous woman," he added.

Dr. Cory didn't seem surprised.

"She's not going anywhere," he said in reply to Tom.

Tom excused himself and in a few minutes was facing the town marshal, and looking at a man in the back cell who Tom supposed was the infamous Frenchie.

A small man, he had a small beaky nose, and a lot of wrinkles for his age. He looked about thirty-five.

After telling the marshal who he was, Tom told him the whole story, again leaving out the family part about the letter and just saying how he was searching for his brother Will and what had happened since. He talked quietly, so Frenchie couldn't hear.

Casey's Journey   115

"I don't have a problem with letting you talk to Frenchie, as long as I can listen," the marshal said.

As Tom walked back toward the cell, the marshal pulled up two chairs a good distance from the bars. He motioned for Tom to sit, and he sat down himself.

Tom decided to get right to the point. He could think of only one thing that made sense of what had happened.

He decided to use the element of surprise. And he would not underestimate Frenchie.

"Hello, Rowan," Tom said, trying to make his voice as low-key and friendly as possible.

Frenchie's expression changed to one of surprise. "Who told you that?"

"It's not important. What is important is that I, oddly enough, am here to try to save your skin."

Frenchie decided to play it smug and confident. "Last I knew, it wasn't a hanging offense, beatin' on a woman. After all, it's not like I stole somebody's *horse!*" he said, chuckling at his own humor.

"What about the two women found dead at your house near the Zeigler mine?"

"What?"

"The Zeigler mine. You remember your wife, surely?" Tom said.

"I didn't do that! I didn't harm her!" Frenchie said.

"I didn't say you did."

Tom let that sink in.

"What do you want?" Frenchie said, all pretense at cockiness gone. Just anger left, and maybe some wariness and sadness, Tom thought.

"Two things. First, the truth about what happened.

And second, for you to tell me about the man that Anna says is left somewhere, still tied up in the woods."

"Why should I tell you that? You the law?" He looked at the marshal. "He the law?"

The marshal didn't answer, an unreadable look on his face, so that after a few seconds, Frenchie looked back to Tom for an answer.

"You runnin' this show?" Frenchie said belligerently to Tom.

Tom said, "I guess so. How about telling the truth for once, Frenchie. Save yourself from a noose around your neck for the murder of your wife and your sister-in-law."

"What makes you think I didn't do it?" Frenchie said suspiciously.

"One, they were shot." Tom decided to leave out the part about knowing about Will's gun.

"Two, I think you beat up Anna because she shot and killed your wife. Hitting women is not your style."

"How'd you know all that?" Frenchie said. "You seem to have a handle on what happened."

"What *did* happen?"

Frenchie scratched hard at his scalp, and then began his story.

"Well, almost a week ago, a man from the Zeigler mine rode up to the house. Name of Will Casey. Worked for the mine owner. Accused me of something—I forget what—"

That was a lie but Tom let that go, purposely.

Frenchie scratched near the crown of his head again, rumpling his hair worse than it already was, and con-

Casey's Journey

tinued, "Anyways, that day, Cora and Leslie had been having a disagreement with Anna again. Casey arrived right in the middle of a big row they were having.

"Leslie and Cora always said Anna wouldn't do her fair share of the chores and although Casey would have never let *me* near enough to get his gun"—here Frenchie grinned regretfully—"Anna ran behind Will as if to gain protection from the other two women. Sure enough, Will put his arms out and let her run behind him for protection.

"An' danged if the little witch didn't pull Casey's gun from behind and shoot Leslie and Cora." He sighed a deep sigh, and looked for a moment as if he would get more emotional, but he didn't.

Death was a thing that was too familiar in his life to show weakness about, it seemed.

Tom guessed that he had loved Leslie, and that that was the reason that, "stone-cold sober," he had lost his temper and beat up Anna, the murderess.

To verify this in front of the marshal, Tom said, "Why did you beat Anna up?"

Frenchie looked down at the floor and said, "Me an' Leslie, we go back fifteen years together."

He looked back up at Tom and said, "What's goin' to happen to me?"

"I guess that depends on whether Anna dies or not, and whether the man you left tied up back in the woods is all right."

"Anna made me take him with us. She said we couldn't leave him there to tell what happened. And we knew that most likely Casey would be blamed if we disappeared, seein' that the women were shot with his gun.

"An' I thought if I stayed, they might blame me for the murders, so I left with Anna, though I didn't never turn my *back* on her for one minute, 'cause she kept Casey's gun.

"I think Anna had a soft spot for Will Casey, though, because of the fact that he *did* put out his arms to protect her an' all. So she didn't kill him—just tied him up and took him with us. Casey is two miles outside of town. Head straight north toward the point of the highest mountain out back. Can't miss him."

Tom let out a big sigh of relief. He couldn't stand waiting any longer. He had this terrible sense of urgency. And dragging information out of Frenchie had taken so long....

There was silence.

The marshal stood up and picked up his chair, indicating that the discussion was over.

Tom stood up, picked up his own chair, and followed the marshal back to the front of the jail near the desk.

"Marshal, I guess you can take over from here. Would you take care of getting a message to Texas Harper and to the people at the Zeigler mine that Will Casey is cleared of the murder of the two women?"

The marshal nodded. "Be glad to."

"What will happen to Frenchie and Anna?" Tom asked, hurriedly.

"Depends. Depends on whether Anna makes it. Doc says no, she's not. Frenchie is off the hook for Leslie and Cora, but ironically, he'll probably get his neck stretched for Anna's death. Say, why did you call him Rowan?"

"Texas Harper says that that's his real name: Rowan Abermarle."

"He's not Frenchie—how do you say that, Malebolge?"

He was torn between telling this man what he knew and wanting to rush out and find Will. He decided to talk quickly.

"That's how I knew Frenchie was not a stupid man. The name he picked to go by is the name only a well-educated or very smart man would choose. It's from an Italian book, a classic called Dante's *Inferno*. Malebolge is the eighth circle of punishment in Hades. The 'Inferno' contains ten bolgi."

"What in tarnation are 'bolgi'?"

"Pits."

"Like peach pits?"

"No, like deep holes in the ground. Punishment holes."

Tom didn't say it, but he remembered from his classical schooling in Greek and Roman literature that the malebolge was a place that punished those who committed acts of fraud. Not murder.

He walked over to the door.

Maybe Texas was wrong about the murders on the Ohio. Frenchie considered himself guilty only of fraud, Tom guessed, by the name he had given himself. Maybe it was his brothers, or the women, who were the actual murderers.

Tom guessed that Frenchie preferred the malebolge

to burning eternally. At the very least, he had picked his name with a sense of irony.

The marshal was not through talking. Tom had a hard time waiting as the marshal continued.

"Well, then, I guess he's some smart, I reckon. Pickin' a name from a thing like . . . like *that*. Not too smart to swing from the limb of a cottonwood tree, though, if Anna dies."

"I'm going to ride out and find Will now," Tom said.

"You want me to ride along?"

"No."

"Appreciate it if you'd check back with me and let me know how you make out," the marshal said.

"I'll do that."

As he shut the door of the marshal's office behind him, Tom felt a terrible need to hurry. All of this seemed to be taking so long, when what he really wanted was to just find his brother from the moment he heard what Anna was saying. And he felt even more in a hurry when Frenchie had said where Will was.

Chapter Fifteen

It was not as easy as he thought. Tom headed off into the trees using the highest point of the largest mountain as his guide. The trouble was, as soon as he was in the high trees, he could no longer see the point.

He thought of the first few lines from Dante's *Inferno*

> *Midway on our life's journey,*
> *I found myself in dark woods,*
> *the right road lost.*

It was odd that the poem didn't say *"my* life's journey," but *"our,"* as if it included Will's.

He could only depend on his and Blacky's ability to go straight, which was not so easy as they continually had to go around pine tree trunks blocking their way.

Unfortunately, the trees didn't have any discoloration, or moss growing on them to help him go straight north. He and Blacky just did the best they could and continued on.

When he felt that he had gone two miles, he began to branch out, cutting wide circles to try to find Will.

Worse, although it was a couple of hours till dusk, it would get dark sooner among these tall trees in front of the mountain. Tom didn't want Will to spend another night, helpless, tied up in the woods without food and water.

He smiled wryly to himself. All he had to eat was more of the dang jerky in his saddlebag. But if Will was hungry enough, that would have to do.

He began to call out, "Will! Will Casey!" as he rode. Then he listened to hear if there was any answer.

Finally, he rode left as he thought he heard an answering thumping noise. He was right!

There, a few yards away, was Will, tied to a tree trunk, his mouth stuffed with a dirty brown silk bandanna tied tightly around his jaw, and with his legs and arms bound with rope.

Will, bless his fighting spirit, had managed to lift his legs high enough to bring them down on the ground hard enough to make a thumping noise!

Will was almost crying as Tom, his fingers shaking, struggled to untie the slippery silk. The knots were tied tight. He was tempted to try to cut them with a knife but he was afraid that he would cut Will.

There, he had the knot loosened! In another minute he had Will's mouth free.

He used his knife to cut Will's chest free from the tree trunk, and then cut Will's arms and legs free.

Will made no attempt to rise. He evidently was too numb from being tied so tightly. He began rubbing his legs to try to get the circulation back in them.

"Tom!" Will said. "How did you find me? I had just about given up. Last night, I was so frightened—an animal came in the night and sniffed me. I was so afraid that tonight the animal would return."

"It's a long story. We have time for that later," Tom said as he removed a canteen from the saddle. He removed the cap and handed it to Will.

Will knew enough to take only small sips.

Tom squatted beside him, feeling very relieved that he had found Will alive.

"Do you know about that woman, Anna?" Will asked, his voice shaking a little.

"Sorry to say that I do," Tom said, putting his arm around Will's shoulder as he tried to stand up on his stiff legs.

"A woman ... murdering!" Will said. "I still can't believe it! She and Frenchie went into town to get supplies ... we better watch out! They may come back. She said they would be back for me."

"I don't think you need worry about that," Tom said.

He helped Will up on Blacky.

"She let her guard down, I guess, and Frenchie let her have it. He beat her up pretty badly for killing his wife. She may not live."

"What about Frenchie? He's dangerous, too."

"In jail."

"Where's my gun?"

"The marshal has it, I think."

Will looked very relieved. Tom had never seen him so close to crying, even during the war.

Tom didn't have the heart to tell him about the letter—about why he was looking for him in the first place. At least right now. He decided to joke to break the tension.

"*Little* brother, do I *always* have to come and rescue you?" he said, looking up at his brother, now on the horse.

It was two jokes in one, for Will was a good two or three inches taller than Tom. And he had grown in width. His legs looked as thick as small tree trunks. And a few times during the war, they had each come to each other's rescue.

The last time Tom had seen Will they were both half-starving, at the end of the war. Red, Tom, Will, and Ben had taken turns going out in the nearby woods hunting for squirrel, rabbit, anything, but it was usually only Tom, and once in a while Ben, who returned with anything edible.

The four of them had made jokes about it.

"What now?" Will said, smiling at the joke. It had worked, because Tom detected a mood change in Will. That was good.

"If you want your gun back today, we go and see the marshal."

Tom swung up on Blacky behind Will.

"I do."

"Let's go get it, then," Tom said. "It'll be dark soon."

As they rode, Tom handed Will some jerky.

"Does the marshal know that I didn't kill those women?"

"He does." Tom added, "He's promised to notify a lawman named Texas Harper, back in Lame Horse Canyon, that you're innocent. Texas is a good man. And he's going to get a message to the people at the mine what happened."

As they rode into town, Tom saw that people were lined up on both sides of the street, watching them. They rode up in front of the marshal's office and Will slid down off Blacky and tied her to the hitching rail.

Together they went inside, and in a few minutes they were back outside with Will's gun.

"You reckon my horse is in the stable?" Will asked.

"Won't know, little brother, until we go and see," Tom said, grinning.

A big chestnut was in the stable and he nickered when he saw Will. He looked well cared for.

"That there your horse?" a cranky old man said, rising from where he was sitting on a chair out of sight in an empty stall near the door. A dim oil lamp was the only light available, hanging from a large hook on the wall.

"Yes."

"Figgered a nice piece of horseflesh like that didn't belong to nobody like Frenchie," the man said. "Been here a while. That'll be two dollars."

Will looked at Tom. Obviously, the Malebolges—Frenchie and Anna—had not overlooked robbing Will as he was tied up.

Tom looked at Will and grinned, then reached into

his pocket and took out the money and handed it to the man.

"You come up with that so easy, maybe I shoulda asked for three," the man joked.

"You charge quite a lot," Will said.

"Need to make up fer those who sneak out and get away without payin'," the old man said. "I'm too old to run after them, an' the crooked ones know it."

Will led the chestnut horse outside and mounted up.

"Get down off that horse," Tom said, in a joking manner. "Whatever you've got planned can wait. *Everything* can wait. I need some food in my belly."

Will dismounted, chuckling. He lead the chestnut over to where Tom's horse was tied on the darkened street. He tied the chestnut next to Blacky.

"Sorry, I forgot. You gave me the jerky to eat on the way into town. What would Mother say to hear you talking that way? Belly? Food in your belly? She'd say that that was vulgar. 'You need to call it stomach, dear,' she'd say. 'Or better yet, dear, don't mention undelicate parts at all.' "

"You forget I lived in Texas for a couple of years," Tom said as he grinned at Will. "I need to hunker down over some grub," he said deliberately.

Will grinned back. "Guess I could hunker down over some myself."

Will patted Tom's shoulder in a reassuring way and they walked up the street to Tyler's Restaurant and went inside.

Chapter Sixteen

Forty minutes later Will was rubbing circles on his stomach, saying, "I ate too much. I feel like I'm gonna bust."

"I told you not to eat that last stack of hotcakes," Tom said jokingly.

He was feeling very happy that he had found Will and that everything was working out all right. At least as far as the murders of the two women went.

The other problems still needed to be dealt with. Like the letter from home.

How could he bring it up now, after Will had been kidnapped and tied up in the woods all night, and accused of murder? Not to mention what had happened to him during the war, and afterward, at home, dealing with David and their mother.

He just hoped that Will didn't hate him for leaving, for running out west looking for Angus Brown, Jr.

And for staying on in Texas and working on the

horse ranch after the months and months of fruitless searching had turned up nothing.

He got up, left the table, and walked over to the waitress and took care of the bill. He talked with her for a few minutes and arranged for her to pack some additional food. Then he walked back over to where Will sat at the red-checkered tablecloth near the front window of the restaurant.

The waitress returned shortly with the burlap bag of food that he had arranged for. She handed it to Tom.

Matching red-checkered curtains covered more than halfway up the windows so, Tom suspected, no one could see in well enough to shoot anyone through the windows.

After the waitress left their table she began to prepare to close up the restaurant. He and Will stood up, and walked outside. The town looked deserted.

Tom was unsure what to do next, but Will seemed to have something in mind as he walked directly to their horses at the hitching post down the street.

Will swung easily up into the saddle of his chestnut horse and turned the horse facing back the way Tom had originally come into town.

"I need to talk to you," Will said, "but the morning is soon enough."

Tom nodded and mounted up, and he followed Will out of town, puzzled.

Just outside of town, Will reined in and got down off his horse near where a gray boulder the size of a small house loomed in the darkness.

A creek ran nearby, and Tom let Blacky drink, and then picketed him. Later, he gave him some oats.

Casey's Journey

The chestnut had just been cared for in the stable, so they unrolled their bedrolls, and although Tom wanted to talk to Will, he knew that Will had had a hard few days, and needed sleep more than talk right now.

In the morning, Tom opened the bag that the woman had given him and they ate the cold biscuits and ham slices that she had packed. Just being with Will again made Tom very happy.

Tom waited to hear what it was Will had to say about why he was in Arizona Territory, and about what had happened at home.

Instead, Will surprised Tom as they finished their last bites of breakfast: "Okay, out with it," Will said unexpectedly. "I know that you didn't come all this way because of the murders, since you obviously had to leave weeks ago from where you were to get here, and the murder business only happened in the past week. Was it because you heard the same thing that I did, that Angus Brown is near here?"

"What?" Tom said. "Angus Brown?"

Will seemed puzzled by Tom's reaction.

"Isn't that why you're here?" Will said. "Didn't you notice that I didn't seem that surprised to see you?"

"Actually, no," Tom said truthfully. "I had other reasons for being here."

"Other reasons?"

"Yes. I'll tell you about that in good time, but tell me—Angus Brown is near here?"

"Both Angus Browns. Junior and senior. I was working for a couple of weeks at the mine to get enough money to buy ammunition and supplies to go and search him—them—out."

Will looked at Tom and said, "By the way, how much more money do you have? We can leave right now if you have enough for supplies and such."

Tom did. He had three hundred dollars in a small leather pouch in his pocket, and thirty dollars hidden in his saddlebags. But he wanted to know more about what was what, first.

"Where are they?"

Will grinned. "With your new Western-style, ungenteel way of talking, don't you mean where is that egg-sucking, no-good, dang-blasted Yankee officer and his no-good egg-sucking son?"

"Okay, yes," Tom said, grinning back. At least Will still had a sense of humor, a sign that maybe his mother and David were wrong about Will's being suicidal.

A man who can joke can usually make it through life, Tom had noticed. At least, most of the time.

Tom was relieved.

"The good news is that General Brown is no longer a general. He's only a captain. Messed up somewhere in his career—now, this is only gossip, so I don't know if that's true or not. Seems that a reduction like that would be highly unusual. If not impossible.

"There was some news about him recently that made his name get in the papers. I haven't been able to find out what it was.

"Anyway, the part of the news I heard that *seems* to be true is that Brown, senior, was assigned to Fort

Lewis six months ago. It's a fort that was built shortly after the war, on the edge of the desert.

It's in a direct line southwest of here. It was built in 1865 to protect the miners and settlers down there against the Apaches. He brought his wife and his no-good son with him. Seems Angus, Jr., has had trouble holding a job. So he's still living at home."

Angus Brown, Senior and Junior! Southwest of here!

"What was it that you were going to tell me?" Will said.

"I need time to think," Tom said, digging in his pocket for his money pouch. He handed Will the leather pouch.

"Well, I guess you haven't changed much, then," Will said jokingly. "You always needed time to think."

"Take this. Go back into town, if you don't mind, and buy us some supplies—whatever you think we need."

He waited until Will rode off, and then he quickly searched in his saddlebags for some paper on which to write a message. After silently grieving a minute, he wrote rapidly:

Dear Will,

I can't express how happy I am to have seen you and spent this time with you. But we have different things we need to do. Enclosed is a letter from David. You need to go home and make peace with Mother. I will take care of both the Angus Browns. On this, I give you my word. I can only promise that I will do as I see fit. Use the money to get home. If you need to write me, you can send it care of Red Duffield, our old friend who is in Sante Fe now. That is where I will go after I take care of the Browns. I know that you could never be a spy for the North. David is an obnoxious fool. Take care of yourself. Come back here if you can, to Lame Horse Canyon. With my highest regards, good-bye for now.

Tom

With a quick glance up at the sky to make sure that there was no sign of rain, Tom put the two letters together, and put a gray rock on them to keep them secure. He checked to make sure they were easily visible when Will returned, right in front of the large boulder.

If he was lucky, he would have an hour's head start, by the time Will returned from town.

He had only what was left from what the waitress had put in the bag to eat. That, and the jerky, would have to do.

The supplies would slow Will down and there was no way that Will's large but more delicately built chestnut could catch up to Tom's sturdy horse.

He was off, covering ground quickly, as soon as he took one look back, regretfully, with a lump in his throat, toward where Will—decent, honest, trusting Will—had disappeared from sight.

He grieved that he had seen his youngest brother for such a short time.

Chapter Seventeen

The trip back down through "Paradise Canyon" was less pleasant, for now Tom was hurrying down the steep, twisting trail, which made it more dangerous. Once again, he was grateful for Blacky's surefootedness.

Once he was back out of the canyon, the rest of the trip southwest was uneventful, but lonely.

He missed Will. It was a cruel twist of fate that having located him, he now had to leave him so soon, but he didn't want Will in any more trouble—or danger. He'd just been through enough.

The heat increased as he traveled south. The land was gradually going downward. Each afternoon, he had to worry about the thunderstorms that came up. He was out in the open here, which added to the danger.

As the fort came into sight on the morning of the fourth day, it was not as he expected it to look. Spanking clean, white, well-built wooden buildings in neat rows with unexpectedly large windows sat around a large open rectangle of grass.

The fort was set in an area with one side toward a mountain toward the north. The road came upon the fort from the southwest, circling up and around a ridge so that he was looking north toward the mountain behind the fort, and east to see the whole thing.

Toward the south was a treeless ridge of land that stretched on out of sight behind the town area.

The land sloped down on both the west and east sides of the fort, so in effect it was sitting on tableland.

As he came up the trail on the sloping ridge, he came upon the first group of buildings—the town—just outside the fort.

The town buildings were in a neat row on both sides of the street, and although they weren't all painted the bright clean white of the buildings of the fort, they were all neat and sedate and looked well cared for. Certainly a contrast to the slapdash buildings of Betty and the mining buildings.

Here, there were no empty whiskey bottles in the street or between the buildings, and there was no trash anywhere to be seen, as if the discipline of the fort also stretched to the townspeople here.

He had arrived about 4:00 and what he planned to do here couldn't be done until late night. He tied Blacky to a hitching rack and went inside a restaurant.

Inside, a waitress was softly singing "Listen to the Mockingbird" to herself as she swept the floor. The place was empty except for himself. She came over and said, "What can I do for you?"

Casey's Journey

A strand of light-brown hair had fallen out of her bun and was hanging near her mouth. She pursed her lips and blew the hair out of the way as she spoke. When that didn't work, she tucked the stray hair behind her right ear, instead.

She didn't wait for him to answer, saying, "Frijoles, beans, beef, biscuits. What's yer pleasure?"

"A lot of each, and coffee."

"Comin' right up."

When she returned with the coffee, he said to her, "This is not what I had pictured in my mind. The fort, I mean. I thought that there would be stockade walls. Not just a bunch of well-kept buildings sitting on a flat section of land on a ridge."

She chuckled. "Why would any Indian with half a brain attack a fort full of soldiers with rifles and pistols? It's the freight wagons heading toward the mining areas, bringing in supplies, and the settlers' wagons, that the Indians attack. And believe me, Apaches are anything but stupid! "After you eat, go out and take a look around if you like. In Arizona we're hospitable, with a few exceptions," she said, smiling.

"I might do that," he said. "The fort looks quite impressive."

"Supposed to be," she said. "To scare the dickens out of the Indians. Show them how rich and powerful the U.S. government is."

After he ate, he walked back outside.

The fort was impressive. He knew enough about the U.S. Army to know what he was looking at.

Closest to the town's main street was a series of

corrals and a large hay yard with hay for the army's horses.

The quartermaster's storehouse, some shops, and the hospital matron's quarters were also on the south side of the fort in the first row of neat buildings.

In a second, small row were two small buildings by themselves. One was the magazine and the other a bathhouse.

Another line of buildings consisted of a hospital, the commissary, and a group of buildings housing most of the soldiers, called the company quarters.

By themselves, facing inward, at the far end of the parade ground were just two buildings, first the laundry building and then the important one—the administration building.

Along the far north area, with their backs toward the mountain in the distance behind the fort, stood the row of buildings that most interested Tom.

These buildings had the best view of the mountains out the back windows. These buildings had yards and gardens behind the houses. Here, in this neat line, were the doctor's quarters, then closer, a couple of married officers' quarters, then the commanding officer's quarters, and then the bachelor officers' quarters.

It was the commanding officer's quarters that interested Tom. The house was large, a two-story rectangular house with a kitchen jutting out the back.

It was the second house in from the administration building at the far left end of the parade ground.

No one bothered Tom, or even seemed to notice him as he walked around. It was late in the afternoon and things seemed to be very calm.

Casey's Journey

The commanding officer's quarters was a house that was opulent compared to the rest of the buildings, as befitted his status.

The commanding officer of a fort usually made about $150 a month, Tom knew. Maybe even more out here. Because of this, the commanding officer could afford to bring his family with him.

Regular soldiers made about $13 or so a month. Their pay had been cut since the war.

Tom had looked at enough so that he could make his plans for later. He stopped in Sullivan's General Store to buy oats, coffee, bacon, and hardtack, although he had hated hardtack since the war.

He watered Blacky at a watering trough in front of the store.

Then he headed south, away from the fort.

When he was a reasonable distance out of town, keeping an eye out for Apaches, he found a place where there was a clump of three cedars in a low area that must collect water during rain.

Here, he and Blacky were out of sight of town, and hopefully, of Apaches. He unsaddled Blacky, to give him a rest.

He sat, trying to plan what to do, now that he had carefully looked over the fort. But his mind kept wandering, going back to his schooling.

Was his mind trying to tell him something?

Why was he all of a sudden thinking back to the tutor his parents had hired? Mr. Bledsoe, who was in charge of their schooling.

One day Mr. Bledsoe had handed him a book about

Goethe, the German writer and poet. David had laughed when Tom pronounced the name Go-eeth.

Mr. Bledsoe gently told him that the name was pronounced Gurr-ta. Mr. Bledsoe had said that one of the good things he felt about Goethe was that Goethe had a largely optimistic view of life. Why was he thinking of that *now?*

One of the things that Tom remembered Goethe had written was *"Boldness has genius, power, and magic to it."*

Mr. Bledsoe had explained that in this case he didn't think Goethe meant magic in the supernatural sense, but magic as in pleasant, wonderful surprises about reaching your goals in life.

Tom thought about this a little more, as he waited for nightfall near the cedars.

The heat of the day had been much worse here than it was back up in the red rock area, where he had been at a higher elevation.

Near dusk, he gave Blacky some water and then some oats, and then sat back down to rest.

He checked his revolver at least five times, making sure that it was ready and loaded.

He was too anxious to sleep, but he unrolled his blanket and tried to rest.

"Genius, power, and magic."

It helped Tom come up with a plan. It was based on something that he remembered Confederate Colonel John S. Mosby did during the war. Walking up to the house where a Union brigadier general was sleeping, Mosby called out, "Dispatches for General Stoughton."

No one challenged him.

Mosby boldly walked into the large house, and into Union Army Brigadier General Stoughton's bedroom where he said, "General, get up."

The general arose, angrily asking, "What is the meaning of this?"

Mosby said calmly, "You are a prisoner."

And he was. The rest of Stoughton's cavalry was stationed six miles away, lodging in much humbler quarters.

The plan had worked, because no one believed that anyone would have the nerve to walk right into the brigadier general's headquarters like that.

A slight variation of this plan might work because of the surprisingly open layout of the fort. At least, Tom had seen enough of the fort to believe it would.

Now that he knew what he was going to do, it seemed to take forever to get just to midnight. Finally, when it seemed certain that it was well past that hour, Tom saddled up.

He rode up to the south side of the fort behind the town. He stopped and picketed Blacky well outside of the sight of the fort, behind the row of stores. It was well out of listening range of a horse's hooves.

Quietly, and furtively, he made his way through the town area and on over to the fort.

As far as where the outhouses were located, he was fairly safe. Men were going back and forth between the barracks and the latrine all night in the dark, and suspicions would not be very much aroused to see a man walking in that area.

Past that, he was on his own not to be spotted by a guard.

Although the moon was not full, the hot summer night was not pitch-black, but a lighter blue-black. There was a bright half moon. He could see the shapes of things clearly.

Lights were still on here and there about the fort.

He was surprised, even though there were a number of guards about, how easy it was to actually make his way to the commanding officer's house. The guards appeared to be watching the supply buildings, the magazine, and the horses more than the buildings that people were in.

There was a guard watching the commanding officer's house, but Tom needed only to watch a few times how long it took the guard to circle the fairly large building. It was a hot night, and the guard was walking slowly.

Because it was still hot, the large second-floor windows were all open.

He waited for the next time the guard approached and passed by.

Then Tom shinnied up the pole at the corner of the porch and lay down flat on the roof, timing it so that he lay completely still as the guard passed by down below.

As the guard made the next round, he carefully looked in the two open windows available to him on the roof.

As the guard made the third round, he slipped in through the open window on the right. It was obviously a sewing room, but because it was dark, Tom couldn't make out much else.

He took his revolver out and crept into the front bedroom down the hall on the left. Brown and his wife were sleeping on their backs.

A little bit of moonlight shone into the room.

Luckily, he saw the wife was on the inside of the bed toward the window and Brown was on the side nearest the door.

His large belly made a small mountain under the covers.

Tom stuck his revolver's barrel gently on Brown's temple, and slowly, sleepily, the man opened his eyes.

It worked as Tom had planned, as he wanted to wake the man gently so as not to wake up the wife.

For the first few seconds, Brown thought it was just a fly that had landed on his face.

Then, when he fully opened his eyes, he saw Tom. Tom held a finger to his lips to indicate silence.

Brown moved his head slightly to indicate agreement, and he rose out of the bed. His white nightshirt fell below his knees.

As Brown arose, his wife rolled over, facing the window. She made a soft noise as she rolled, but she appeared to be asleep and didn't move after that.

Moving the revolver from Brown's temple, he now pointed it into the middle of Brown's back.

As they left the room, Tom indicated silently that Brown should close the door. He did, obviously knowing how to shut it without waking his wife.

As they went down the hall, Tom reentered the sewing room, and said softly to Brown, "Shut the window. And be quiet about it."

"May I light the lamp?" Brown said.

"You want to see my face?" Tom said.

"Not particularly," Brown said. "But I didn't have time to get my glasses, and my night vision isn't so good anymore."

"Light it, then," Tom said.

This wasn't going exactly as Tom had planned. He walked over himself and shut the door to the sewing room. Then he went over and shut the window as Brown was struggling to light the oil lamp.

He had planned on shooting the man as soon as he found out where Angus Brown, Jr., was, and letting the old man know *why* he was here. Letting him know just exactly *why* he was going to kill Angus Brown, Jr.

But Brown was not the arrogant man he had expected. There was something already defeated and small about him.

Under different circumstances, Tom might have felt sorry for him. He suspected that Brown had been sent here as a punishment, to get rid of him. Perhaps he had covered up for his rotten son once too often.

"Get away from the window," Tom said forcefully, once the lamp had been lit.

Brown did, sitting in a rocking chair in the corner on the right side of the room. Near the rocking chair was a quilting frame and a piece of a blue-and-white quilt stretched on it. Someone in the house used this room for quilting.

Tom was careful to stay out of sight of the window.

Casey's Journey

He moved to the left side of the room opposite the rocking chair. The window was between them.

"Do you know who I am?" Tom said. "And why I'm here?"

"To kill me, I guess. Who you are, I have no idea."

"Do you remember Benjamin Casey?"

"Who?"

"Benjamin Casey."

Brown shook his head in bewilderment.

"I haven't a clue. So many things . . ." His shoulders dropped and he sighed, resignedly.

"What?"

"So many things have happened. Are you one of the men who lynched my son?"

"What?"

"I said, are you one of the men who lynched my son?"

"Lynched your son!"

"I guess you're not. You seem surprised. So I guess you're not. Then why are you here? To kill me? What did my son do to you? Was someone you know one of the people he bushwhacked? If you are, I'm sorry. I had no idea he was doing that, I assure you."

"Bushwhacked?"

It took Tom a few seconds to fully comprehend.

"What in the living blazes are you talking about?" Tom said. He waved his revolver at Brown in a warning fashion, but Brown didn't seem to care.

"You better start from the beginning, and tell me what is going on," Tom said, narrowing his eyes in warning at Brown, his finger tense on the trigger of the revolver in his hand.

"About two months ago—we'd been here, Angus and my wife and I, about six months—people started turning up dead outside of town. Bushwhacked—shot in the back, and robbed."

"Ambushed?"

Brown nodded. His eyes were cast down as if he needed to study the floorboards.

"At first we thought it was Apaches. But it wasn't long before suspicion settled on my son."

Tom knew only too well that Angus was Brown's only son.

"I tried to . . ." The man put his head down, and was silent a minute or two.

Brown pulled a bit of material from his white, wrinkled nightshirt to wipe his face, and Tom knew that the man was wiping tears away.

He thought of Ben's young body lying there with a bullet through his chest, his gray Confederate jacket stained with blood, and he wasn't sorry for Brown.

Harshly, he said, "You should have done something about your son long ago. You've known what he was like—a no-good killer—for years. I blame you as much as him for the death of my brother. My brother was the one who Angus, junior killed below Richmond. He knew very well that Lee surrendered on April ninth. The war was over. He killed my brother on April tenth. For no reason."

"I'm sorry." Brown looked up with a sad face.

"I'm afraid sorry doesn't bring my brother back to life."

"Why blame me for what my son did?"

"You looked the other way when you saw what

your son was capable of. You made excuses for him, never held him accountable. If a boy's father won't hold him accountable, who will?"

"But he was . . . sick."

"So you just protected him and let him continue?" Tom said bitterly.

"I . . . tried," Brown said.

"That's not good enough. It's wrong, morally, to look away from knowledge like that. You knew he was a murderer and you didn't do anything about it! You're in the U.S. Army! You're supposed to be honorable! I shouldn't have to tell you a thing like that!"

Brown said, "I . . . I . . ." Then he gave up, putting his head in his hands and looking down so that Tom couldn't see his face.

But Tom didn't relent.

He'd had to hold this terrible anger inside him for too long.

"There was a man who came and told me that your son was running away to Texas. And that you were after me, and always would be until I was caught."

Brown looked up, surprised.

"I sent that man. I'd heard that you'd vowed to get Angus. I sent Angus to relatives in Illinois. And I figured that you would be safe in Texas."

"Safe! Thinking that someone was after me all these years? Unable to go home? Watching my back all this time? What in tarnation is the matter with you?"

Brown had tricked him! Sent him on a wild goose chase.

"You're a wretched excuse for a human being!" Tom said.

Brown put his head down in his hands again.

"I know that. I've made mistakes—"

"Made mistakes! You excuse your own mistakes as easily as you let your son off! Made mistakes!" No wonder his son was the way he was!

Tom shook his head. "You disgust me."

"Are you going to kill me?"

"No. I wouldn't waste one of my bullets on a man like you."

He let that sink in, although he sensed it was hopeless talking to a man whose thinking processes were so mucked up, so pathetically inadequate.

"You say that your son was lynched?"

Brown nodded. "A bunch of men tracked him and—"

"Good riddance, I say."

Brown was silent, and made no movement, except for his shoulders going up and down as he breathed.

"Do you want to know where the body is buried?" Brown said, looking up at Tom.

"No. This is ended. Right now. Understand?" He meant that when he left the fort tonight, no one would be sent after him.

Brown understood exactly what Tom meant.

Brown stood up and walked toward the door. Tom waited as Brown opened the door, and then Tom blew out the oil lamp, opened the window, and slipped out in case Brown should change his mind and sound an alarm.

It was silent as Tom watched for the passing of the guard, then hung down off the corner of the porch and dropped quietly to the ground. He crept back across the same area, following the same path as he had used when he came.

Reaching Blacky, he swung up on his horse and rode west out around the fort, making a wide loop, before he started northeast in the moonlight.

He figured putting some distance between himself and the fort was a wise thing to do.

Chapter Eighteen

Because Will hadn't followed him and shown up at the fort, Tom figured that Will had gone east, back home as Tom had asked him to in the letter to him.

That left one more thing for Tom to do: to find out the truth, if he could, about the spy business that Will had been accused of.

If Tom wasn't the spy, and Will wasn't the spy, who was? Red Duffield? Ben? Tom thought not.

Ben had been raised by Poppa to be loyal. All four boys had been raised to be loyal. Whether your family, or your state or the country was right or wrong, you were loyal to them.

The North had been like a bossy older brother, telling the South what to do and what not to do. Of course the South had the right to secede.

Bossy older brothers are not always right, bullying their way because they are bigger and stronger, like David.

Casey's Journey

And they hadn't been right this time, had they?

Had they?

The more he'd thought about it in the last few years, he realized that the North had fought because of the issue of slavery. And Tom did think slavery was wrong. But that was not what he'd thought that they were fighting about. Hadn't General Lee said that they were fighting for the right to secede if they wanted to? To be their own bosses and set their own fates without the North butting in?

What right did the North have to decide that they were the boss of the whole nation?

Tom knew that he wasn't so sure anymore what was wrong and what was right. But he knew one thing. His parents' way of life was over.

And he knew what he had to do now.

The first thing he needed to do was to get back north to red rock country, and then make some money somehow to head east from there to Sante Fe.

He thought about Red Duffield as he rode. He could see the wagon track trail in the moonlight quite clearly. It had cooled down and was a beautiful night.

Could Red have some answers? Could he have been the spy? Was there really a spy at all?

He rode cautiously, even though it was commonly supposed that Apaches didn't travel at night.

When he was a few hours away from the fort, he rode off to the side of the trail about two hundred yards and camped behind a rise.

When he awoke, it was just after dawn, and soon he was on his way again.

It was quiet the rest of the way back to the red rock

country, although he rode for a few hours alongside a prospector who, although he was very secretive about prospecting information, didn't mind telling what he knew about where canyons and mesas were that had a lot of wild horses in them, free for the taking, he said.

You had to run them down to catch them, he said. Needed a partner or two, and a corral. Not much else, the man said.

He described in detail where these canyons were. They were only an hour or two from the red rock country where Tom was headed, below the one Tom called Paradise Canyon.

Shortly after, the prospector headed off to the right on a trail he said led to the Vulture Mountains.

Tom was relieved when he saw red rocks jutting up in the distance.

He rode past the wagon ruts that were the indication of the road to the Zeigler mine, and traveled toward Lame Horse Canyon.

On the bench outside the jailhouse, sitting on the bench, was Texas Harper. He was fanning his face with what looked like a brand-new black hat.

"Nice hat," Tom said, grinning, as he dismounted.

"Where you been?" Texas said. "Got yer message about your brother and all. Glad to hear you were right about him."

"Thanks," Tom said. "And thanks for helping me."

"Think nothing of it," Texas said, smiling. "Speaking of helping, was it you who helped June Webster with her broken wagon wheel?"

Tom thought for a minute and then remembered that

lady he'd helped. She'd said her name was June Webster, if he remembered it right.

"Yes."

"Came by here the other day. Tole me what happened. I figgered it was you by the description. Right nice of you to do that.

"She was looking for someone to help her, seein' as her brother's so poorly. Asked if you were still around. I said not so's I'd noticed. But I said if I saw you I'd pass on the word that if you're so inclined, she's in need of a body to help her build a small house.

"She's hired one man already." Texas grinned as he looked around. "You remember the gent that was here choppin' wood last time you were hereabouts, don't you? Name was Jake Jameson. He had to promise June Webster to swear off the bug juice until the job is done, though."

Tom chuckled. "Guess I do remember him, at that. I never built anything before, but I'll try anything. I sure hope Jake Jameson knows how to build a house."

"Jake? He's been buildin' things since he was knee-high to a whiskey bottle. Just do like he says and you'll be fine."

"How do I get to the Websters' place?"

"Go back the way you came. Go past the two houses in sight on the left. Then go further until you come to a small new road on the left that leads down into the canyon near the creek. Look careful or you'll miss it."

Tom touched his hat and mounted Blacky. He turned Blacky around and started back along the wagon track trail. Riding up and down this "road" in

Lame Horse Canyon was getting to be a habit. One he could grow to like.

Tom worked for four weeks for the Websters.

The good news was that June Webster seemed to have a way of keeping Jake away from the bug juice. At least so far.

The plank house he and Jake built for her and her brother was small, and sat on a high knoll a good distance back from the creek, in case of flooding in the future.

June Webster was kind and a good cook, and Tom regretted a few times that she was close friends with Jake. She was very devoted to her ill brother. She and her brother seemed to get along well.

Harry Webster was out of sight most of the time, lying in a bed in the wagon that they were living in temporarily until the three room house was built.

Tom was careful to stay away from June Webster, because he knew if he got to know her better he would get attached to her. As it was, she paid very little attention to him.

Evenings, she did most of her talking to Jake. They discussed the house. She told him what she wanted done, and he told her how he could do it best.

One morning, he heard her singing as she did laundry near the creek. She was singing "Oh, Susanna" in a clear, pleasant voice. *She sure is pretty*, he said to himself.

The morning he was ready to leave, he had enough money in his pocket go to Santa Fe. He had the feeling that when Harry Webster passed away—and it seemed it would be soon—Jake would probably marry June Webster.

Tom left Lame Horse Canyon and set out for the other canyon, the one he called Paradise Canyon. There he intended to take the road that wound up and around to the town on the high plateau where he had first found Will.

In some ways, he regretted leaving the kind, pretty woman, but she had her brother and Jake.

And he needed to go to Sante Fe and talk to his old friend Red Duffield and find out about the spy business and clear Will's name.

The canyon road was still as breathtaking. Once again after he wound around and up the switchback trail at the canyon's end, Tom marveled at the pine forest at the top of the canyon. The thick layer of pine needles on the forest floor kept undergrowth from thriving and so the view into the woods and trees was unobstructed.

And again, it was at least twenty degrees cooler on the high plateau. Tom bought a few supplies in Pine Vista and stopped in at the town marshal's office.

Nothing had changed. Anna was still hanging on to life, and Frenchie was still in jail.

The marshal's best guess was that Frenchie would spend time in prison for stealing from the mine and that Anna would be sent to prison for the murders for the rest of her life—if she survived.

Tom rode off to the east, following the trail that led to Santa Fe.

Chapter Nineteen

Tom rode first into an area of mountains shaped like cones. They looked like pictures he'd seen of volcanoes.

Further on, he saw buttes, far, far in the distance. The buttes had stripes of white, pink, and gray running sideways through them. He thought they were a very beautiful sight.

Many areas seemed very desolate, but he saw, off the road in the distance on both sides of the trail, round hogans, some with a few additional buildings nearby. Tom could not help wonder: What did they do for water out here? Obviously, they knew of water sources that he didn't.

Water became a problem, and Tom was grateful every time he ran into a trading post, or indeed, any signs of civilization. He bought a second canteen.

He passed ruins of ancient rock-walled buildings

high on mesa or bluffs, and once he dismounted and walked up to take a closer look at the ruins.

The ruins must be from ancient Pueblo people, such as the Hopi Indians, Tom guessed, because he had heard that the Navajo had round hogans that they lived in during the winter and brush houses during the summer.

As he looked over the rocks, he saw that there were rooms below him. He suddenly had the feeling that he'd better be careful because the logs that made up the ceilings of the rooms below him were certainly centuries old and might cave in at any minute.

The view from the top of the ruins was striking; you could see a great distance in all directions. What did the people do for water here? he wondered as he gazed around. There was no sign of water. Anywhere.

On the way down, he saw a bright green lizard about five or six inches long sitting on a whitish rock. It had a collar of bright red and yellow around its neck, and seemed unafraid of him.

He watched it, fascinated, until it got tired of his looking at it, and scurried off into the grass.

Later, he passed through an area where great trees had turned to solid rock. If someone had told him that such a thing could happen, he would have been tempted to call that person a liar; but then, on this journey, he had seem much that was hard to believe, like a town on such a steep hill as the one near the Zeigler mine, and a fort with no stockade.

Again, thunderstorms rolled through in the afternoons.

When he rode into Santa Fe, it was midmorning. He was amazed at how busy it was. The place was bustling with activity.

A chicken vendor was walking in the large square, with chickens for sale inside a large metal cage on his back.

Mexican men were carrying large wooden buckets of water slung by poles, the buckets swinging as the men walked.

Freight wagons were being unloaded in front of stores, some with bolts of materials, some with whiskey.

Mutton was hanging from the limbs of cottonwood trees that were near the ditch of water running in front of a line of long adobe buildings. He heard someone call it an *acequia:* irrigation ditch.

There were burros loaded with firewood for sale. There were oxen, horses, and mules.

He hadn't seen so many people in a long time.

People all over! Busy, laughing, shouting, scolding, and doing everything that people do in a crowded place.

How was he going to find Red Duffield?

He would have to either ask around, or find each general store and inquire.

Even on the plantation in Virginia when he was a kid, he'd never seen so many things being unloaded! Axes, rifles, barrels labeled tacks, nails, butcher knives, hunting knives, hoes, adzes, cotton and silk threads, hooks and eyes, buttons, needles, pins, spoons, scissors, mirror frames, glass window panes, and so many more things.

Casey's Journey

Mexican blankets and jewelry were being loaded instead of unloaded, obviously going away from Sante Fe, probably back east, Tom guessed. Barrels and boxes were everywhere.

There was dickering going on over mules, burros, and oxen. Silver and gold were changing hands.

Some Mexicans were playing musical instruments over in one corner of a great square, and children were playing games in the shade of cottonwood trees.

Some of the men wore colorful shawls, and he saw some women who had their faces painted with what looked like a flour paste. He guessed it was to protect them from sunburn. No one commented on this, so Tom guessed it was the usual thing.

It was very hot, and the sun shone brightly. Tom could see great mountains, looking pale purple in the distance.

He decided to have something to eat, even though it was early. His food had all but run out, all but the jerky in his saddlebags that he had bought at a trading post, but he was growing sick of jerky.

He found a restaurant that served chili and lamb, and went in and ate heartily. He asked the waitress if she knew Red Duffield, but she looked at him as if he were stupid, and didn't bother to answer.

After, he stopped at a general store and bought supplies for the journey back to Arizona. There was no way of knowing how things would turn out in Santa Fe. He hoped they wouldn't turn out bad.

It was early afternoon by the time he found Red. A man with pure white hair was standing outside one of the stores that stood under the overhang that ran along the strips of adobe buildings.

Tom looked, but had just about decided that it couldn't be Red, when suddenly the man spotted him and yelled, "Tom! Tom Casey, you wicked old goat! Is that you?"

Tom swung down off Blacky and accepted the bear hug that Red gave him as greeting. Tom felt a little sorry as Red hugged him, because it seemed as if Red had shrunk; Tom could feel his bones.

But maybe it was just that Tom, himself, was bigger, on account of all the hard physical labor that had put muscles where they hadn't been before, he thought.

"I'm just about to close up shop for my siesta," Red said. "Wait around about five minutes while I do that and then come home with me, for a bite to eat.

He waited outside, holding Blacky's reins until Red locked up the shop, and then he walked with Red a few blocks to an adobe house.

Red showed Tom around the back of the building, where there was a small corral. They took care of Blacky and went back around to the front of the adobe building.

"Not exactly the Duffield Plantation," Red joked as he went in the small wooden door. Tom almost had to duck as he went inside.

Inside, the walls had been lower part of the adobe walls were painted a yellowish-brown color, while the top half was white.

To the right on the back wall was an adobe fire-

Casey's Journey

place that looked like a beehive. Next to it was a short wall, apparently to block drafts hitting the oven.

Wooden storage shelves, with doors, were hung here and there on the walls in the upper part of the room, and pine storage chests lined the walls. Indian-looking storage baskets were here and there, and looked to be holding food items.

One short table, about a foot high, was in the center of the room. There were no chairs.

A Mexican man and woman, who looked to be in their fifties, were working in the room as Tom and Red entered. They were obviously hired help.

The couple nodded sociably to Red and Tom as they entered, but didn't speak.

The woman was sitting in back of the low table, placing tortillas on a sheet of copper, preparing them for cooking. Behind her on the wall, next to one of the wooden storage shelves, hung strings of chilis, herbs, and a large clay water jug. They hung on rope from the roof rafters, which were peeled logs and poles.

There were rooms to the left and right. The one on the left looked like it was Red's bedroom, and the other, the bedroom of the old couple.

Red didn't appear to be married, then.

Blankets hung over poles which were hung by ropes from the roof rafters, which were also poles. The blankets were red, black, and white, with a little yellow, and added a touch of color and cheer to the sparse furnishings.

Over the doorway into the old couple's bedroom, a

small wooden cross was hung. It was crude, and looked handmade.

When supper was ready, the woman motioned for the three men to sit on the floor around the short table.

Before Red sat down, he opened one of the trunks and took out a couple of papers, opened his shirt, and put them inside. Then he rebuttoned his shirt. He didn't explain why he was doing that, and no one asked.

Red sat down without speaking, and began to eat.

The woman served them roasted corn, tortillas which were used to scoop beans from a large common bowl they all shared, and a hot drink made from what tasted like chocolate. She served the drink from a copper pitcher.

After, Tom and Red walked outside, across the way to where, again, cottonwoods ran near a water ditch. Evidently people used the water ditch for all their water needs. Tom wondered how clean it was, but Red seemed to accept it as the way things were.

"Here, step over the *acequia*," Red said.

Tom did, following Red.

They sat under the cottonwood trees, enjoying the bit of breeze that had arisen.

"So, what can I do for you," Red said.

Tom didn't answer.

Red said, "There were two more battles after *that* day."

Tom didn't need to ask what day Red meant. He knew.

"Blakely, Alabama. Battle was still going on a couple of hours after Lee surrendered. And one in Brownsville, Texas," Red said.

"I know," Tom said. What was Red saying, that it was all right what Angus Brown did?

"Angus Brown, Jr., got himself hung over in Arizona, near Fort Lewis," Tom said.

"No loss to the world," Red said.

Red shifted his body. After a few minutes, he asked, "You have anything to do with it?"

"No. Already done by the time I got there."

"Oh."

There was an awkward silence.

Tom couldn't think of how to bring the subject up. Finally he said, "I want to ask you something." He told Red about the letter from David and what had happened since, leaving nothing out this time.

Red sat, listening. Tom could see that he was apprehensive. Finally, he said to Tom, "You sure you want the truth about that, the spying thing?"

Tom said, "Yes. I do want the truth. I've come a long way for the truth."

"You plannin' on killin' anybody once you find out?"

Tom grinned. "Why, you the spy?"

"Maybe I'll just say I was, an' get your search over with, if you promise me you won't be disappointed."

"Or plug you full of holes," Tom said, smiling at Red. "No. The truth is, I just want to know the truth. Whatever it is—or was. I just want the truth."

Red's mood changed, and he grew more serious.

"Why? It's all over and done with now. Let sleeping dogs lie."

"The dogs aren't sleeping. The rumor about Will caused my family great distress. Caused my father's death, David says."

"David was always a pompous fool, if you'll pardon me for saying that—not that we haven't said that many times before when we were together back then," Red said, chuckling.

"It's not only David. It's caused me, Will, and my mother distress, too."

"You won't like the truth. Maybe it's best to just let it go."

"Like it or not, I want it. And I feel that you can give it to me."

"What will you do after I tell you the truth? Are you going back home to Virginia?"

Tom had done a lot of thinking about this while he was traveling from Arizona to Santa Fe.

"No. I'm going back to Arizona. I'd like to try my hand at catching some of the wild horses that are in the canyons and valleys near Lame Horse Canyon."

He thought of the places that he had seen, what looked like mountains of greenish-gray rock—rocks that looked like they were filled with copper—and who knows what else. He'd like to find out about that.

"I like the red rock country over there," Tom said. "And I like the people. Friendly, decent, hospitable."

"Don't you like it here?" Red asked.

"Too many people. Looks too much like a big city here," Tom said. "I guess I like it where there's wide-open space and just a couple of people at a time."

"Everybody to their own taste," Red said.

"You seem to be doing very well," Tom said.

"Truth to be told, there's a beautiful señorita that I've got my eye on," Red said. "That's why I'm so cautious these days about gettin' shot, even by an old friend.

"After I tell you, are you going to stay the night?"

"Probably not. I think I'll ride out of town this afternoon and spend the night camped out. Kind of gotten used to that."

Tom moved so that instead of sitting alongside Red, he was slightly more across from him. He wanted to be able to see Red's face as Red spoke, to judge whether he believed what Red was saying.

"Let's have it, then," Tom said.

Red stood up. He walked over and leaned against a cottonwood tree trunk. Tom got up and followed him.

Red was hesitant to start, but there, with his face half in the shadows of the leaves, he began: "It was hard for Ben to tell you how he felt. He began to feel that the war was wrong. Wrong for a lot of reasons. Even though I was more your friend than his, he needed someone to talk to, and I listened.

"One of the things that bothered him was the fact that many of the men fighting the war were poor young farmboys. They had never even owned a slave. But they were fighting and dying for the same reason that we—the four of us—were: loyalty to the state of Virginia, and the South. Not because they believed in slavery. But more important, Ben had come to believe that blind loyalty like that is wrong.

"Ben said that a man should do what his own integrity—his *own* beliefs—told him to do."

Tom didn't say anything, but was surprised because

as he had gotten older, he had come to the same conclusion. Blind loyalty. Some things were too complex for that. You need to do your own thinking about things. Slavery was wrong, no matter what he had been taught as a child.

"Ben wanted the war to be over," Red said, taking a cigar out of his breast pocket and lighting it. "And he never came right out and said so, but I think he had come to believe slavery was wrong.

"Want one?" Red said, half-pulling another one out of his pocket.

"No," Tom said. "We all wanted the war to be over.

"It had dragged on so long. And I'll never forget the terrible sight of Richmond burning, as long as I live."

"Me, either. He knew we had no chance of winning. We were just about starving to death," Red said bitterly. "Remember how skinny you were? You were always sneaking part of your food onto Will and Ben's plates. I used to see you do that all the time, when you thought no one was looking."

"They were just kids," Tom said.

"The truth is, I think that Ben tried to hurry up the end of the war by giving information to the Union Army."

"What makes you think that?"

"When Ben was shot that day, you ran into the building right away. I stayed behind with Ben. Ben told me to remove these papers from his haversack." Red unbuttoned his shirt and took out the papers and handed them to Tom.

That was true. Tom remembered clearly that Red had not reached that upstairs room right away. And in his mind, he could still see the anguished look that had been on Red's face. He believed Red so far.

The papers in his hand were in Ben's handwriting, and it did look as if Ben had been passing information to someone in the Northern Army named General Richards. The paper in his hand was about troop movements.

"He probably hadn't bothered to pass this latest information on because we all had heard about Lee signing the peace agreement at Appomattox," Red said.

There were a couple of drops of brown stain on the papers, and Tom guessed that it was Ben's blood. He looked at the drops, and then at Red.

"Did you know about this beforehand?" Tom asked. He felt all choked up.

"Did you know about Ben's spying for the North?"

"No. Not until he told me to take these papers from him so that you and Will wouldn't find them on his body."

He believed him.

"You kept these all this time?"

"Yes. In case you ever came like this and wanted the truth. I'm sorry Will got blamed. None of this was his fault. And I'm sorry about your father. I liked him."

"So did I."

"What are you going to do now?"

"I guess write to my family and tell them that that there was a spy, but it wasn't Will. And that I have seen proof that it wasn't Will. I think they'll take my word for that," he said grimly. "Technically, that's the truth."

Red said, "People have never doubted your word. They'll believe you."

He felt almost sick to his stomach to think of what Ben had done. Had Ben done the right thing?

"If you have no objections, then, I think I'll just put a match to this," Tom said. Red took the cigar from his mouth and handed it to Tom.

"Lit this for just that reason," Red said.

They both watched as the papers caught fire. Tom held them until the flame was in danger of burning his hand, and then he dropped the papers as the last bit curled up into a blackish-white ash.

They both looked at it.

"Well, that's that," Red said. "I, for one, am glad that it's over. I feel like a great weight has been taken off my shoulders. I feel as if I've gone to confession or something."

It was over. Tom felt the same. Angus was dead. Ben was dead that day long ago. There was no one left to tell the story to. Except maybe Will, someday.

Ben had done what his conscience had told him to do. Tom was sure that it had been an agonizing choice for him.

A thought occurred to him. "Did Angus Brown, Junior or Senior, know about Ben's spying?"

Red shook his head, no: "Why would they kill someone who was spying for their side? Besides, they would have no way of knowing. Ben was giving his information to General Richards."

It was true. The papers had been addressed to General Richards.

"I left your name with Will, as a place that he could

get a message to me. Just until I get a place in Arizona. I hope you don't mind," Tom said.

They crossed over the water ditch and back around to the back of the adobe where Blacky was.

"No problem," Red said, as he helped saddle up Blacky. "Let me know where you are and I'll come over a visit," he said.

"Somewhere around Lame Horse Canyon," Tom said. "That's where I'll be. If you get a letter from Will or David, send it there."

"Consider it done," Red said.

They shook hands and Tom mounted up.

It was late afternoon, and he had time to think about all that had happened as he rode.

He realized why it was he liked it out here in the West so much. He would never go back East to live. Out here, the real promise of America existed. The men who wrote the Constitution didn't buy the traditional European idea that birth circumstance alone confers superiority.

That was certainly what his mother clung to, that unearned aristocratic privileges were due to those born to wealth.

It was in Texas, after the war, when he'd first run across people—mostly cowboys—who had very different views than his parents.

In the West, people were judged by their actions. Their birth was not discussed.

Here, you could work hard and rise as far as your own abilities allowed you to go.

It was a much fairer system. In a way, his mother's demanding that her boys get a good education had led to some of her sons—at least Tom and Ben—not believing in the same things she had believed in. It was ironic. He didn't think his mother would like that very much.

Worst of all, he began to think that perhaps he had been wrong. Perhaps the war wasn't so much about the fact that the North was trying to tell the South what to do. Perhaps the war, after all, had really been about slavery. Maybe he and his friends and family had lied to themselves to justify what they were doing.

It was a sobering thought.

He had come a long way. At dusk he unsaddled Blacky, took care of him, and made his camp for the night.

Chapter Twenty

At dawn he was up and continuing on his way back to Arizona.

On the second morning, he noticed two riders about fifteen minutes behind him on the trail.

Sometimes he could see them, other times he just saw the cloud of grayish-white dust they were raising.

He wasn't concerned. This was, after all, the most direct route to northern Arizona Territory from Santa Fe.

Near noon, he stopped to let Blacky rest. He poured some water from his canteen into his hat for Blacky to drink.

The two riders caught up to him, just as he was ready to mount up again.

The two men swung down off their horses near Tom.

If they had pistols, the pistols were concealed in their clothing.

Worse, as he looked over their horses, they appeared to have only one canteen each. That would not do in the waterless land ahead.

The men removed their hats as a sign of respect and politeness, and Tom smiled at them.

"Better put those hats back on, gentlemen," Tom said, "or this sun will roast your scalp inside of fifteen minutes."

The men chuckled, and did what Tom said.

The two men were shorter than Tom, one by an inch or two and the other by quite a bit. The taller one had startlingly blue eyes and black hair. The shorter one had green eyes and light brown hair.

They both looked like they had new clothing on, and fresh haircuts.

When the taller one spoke, Tom had a hard time disguising his surprise; if he did at all.

The man said in an Irish accent, "Goin' to Arizona Territory, are ya?"

Tom nodded. His heart speeded up just the slightest bit. He coughed, to gain time, and to cover up any expression he might have made.

"Dusty out here," he said.

The men nodded.

The shorter one said, "Aye," in an Irish accent.

A plan was forming in his mind of what to say, and he knew he had to appear casual, as if he didn't care one way or the other, for it to work.

"You two Irish?" Tom said innocently.

"Aye. That we are," the tall one said. "I'm Eugene McDowell and this is Joe Duffy."

Casey's Journey 171

There was no reason to hide it anymore, so Tom said, "Tom Casey."

"Would that be a MacCasey or an O'Casey?" the short one, Joe, said.

Tom had to smile. "O'Casey."

Joe Duffy said, "We're from County Roscommon. There were O'Caseys in the south of County Roscommon. Was your family from there?"

Tom shook his head. "I don't know."

"Well, there's a lot of O'Casey clans," Eugene said. "Probably from somewhere else."

He nodded agreement with what the man said.

Tom had to be careful, but he thought he could help James Peake—Boyne.

He said, "It's a small world. Met another Irishman a while back. Oh, maybe about a month ago." He was deliberately lying about when.

A look passed between the two men.

"Oh? Whereabouts?" Eugene said.

"Not near any settlement," Tom said casually. "On the trail, southwest of here. Poor fellow. . . ." Here he decided to make Jim Peake's "death" a dramatic one.

Should he make it by snakebite or by black widow spider bite?

Snakebite sounded more final.

"Poor fellow didn't watch out enough for snakes. Rattler got him. I can't remember his name," Tom said, "What was it?" he said, absently, as if to himself. "Something to do with mountains, I think."

"Was it Peake? James Peake?" Joe said.

"No, I don't think so . . . or maybe . . . yes. I guess that might have been it. I remember it had something to do with mountains . . . yes, I think it was Peake, like mountain peak."

Another look passed between them.

"I can tell you where his grave is, if you like," Tom said, bluffing. "It's about—"

"There's no need for that," Eugene said. "We'll take your word for it."

"How far west are you going? One canteen each isn't enough if you're going far."

The men looked at each other.

"This is as far as we're going," Eugene said. "We would have liked to tell Jim a few things. We got revenge on a man James Peake didn't have much use for. We would have liked to tell him that. We took money from an enemy of Jim's . . . I guess you could call it under false pretenses.

"We used it to come to America to tell Jim something. It's too bad he's dead. He would have enjoyed knowing what we did.

"It was a bit of a delicious payback to a bad, bad, man named MacDermot."

Tom nodded.

"I guess we'll be headin' back to Santa Fe," Joe Duffy said, "and then back to New York City. We're plasterers by trade and there's work for us there. It's too hot here, and there's not enough Irish colleens around."

The two men mounted up.

Joe Duffy looked back just as he picked up the reins with experienced hands, and said with a twinkle in his eye, "If you should be seein' James Peake's 'ghost' anytime soon, tell him he's a free man. Pegeen

MacDermot Peake died five and a half months ago of pneumonia. That's what we came to tell him."

"Nice meetin' you," the two men said, and Joe and Eugene rode off, back toward Santa Fe.

It was then that he remembered that Jim Peake had said that he had come though Santa Fe. And where was it that he said he was going?

The Buell mine, near Buell Crossroads.

He would make sure he sent a message to Jim Peake and tell him that he was a free man. He could do it at Pine Vista.

He mounted up.

The trail was long.

Water and heat were a problem. Thunderstorms helped, but sometimes the nearby strikes of lightning drove him into dips in the land for protection. There, he and Blacky were miserable, waiting out the worst of the lightning strikes and the hard rains.

A few times he passed Navajo herding sheep.

He passed back through the area with the rocks that looked like they had been made from trees, and the place with the buttes in the distance made up of colored stripes of pink, white, and gray.

When he came to the mountains that looked like cones in the distance, he felt that he was coming home. Just over the saddleback in front of him was the settlement. Then there was "Paradise Canyon," and then the Lame Horse area.

He stopped at a trading post and bought bacon and coffee. He had beans and biscuit fixings left from his purchases in Santa Fe.

Then he rode west, over the saddleback which was

the last ridge before Pine Vista, the settlement where Frenchie and Anna were. He debated whether to stop at the marshal's office, but instead just rode over to the mound of graves that was the cemetery.

The simple wooden markers on the two graves told the story. The date on Frenchie's marker was one day after the date on Anna's.

He didn't need to know more. He went to the general store that doubled as a post office, and sent a letter to James Boyne at the Buell Mine, telling him about Joe Duffy and Eugene McDowell, and what they had said about their reason for coming and about the demise of "the dreaded Pegeen."

He rode west, out of the settlement, and then back along the road until he came to the forest on top of the canyon where he had met June Webster and fixed the three broken spokes on her wagon wheel.

Then he rode further and stopped to camp for the night.

He camped at the same place he had camped the night he came through this area first; near the top of the trail that led down into what he still called Paradise Canyon.

He pulled off the trail into the woods, and not wanting to make a fire with all the pine needles around, he made a cold camp, and went to sleep.

Tom woke up excited about the coming day. Although he was almost out of money, he was free.

Free for the first time since the day that Ben was shot, over three years ago, on April 10, 1865. Free from what had been hanging over his head since the war.

Free.

As the realization hit him, he wondered, is this what joy feels like? He had felt it so rarely in his life that he wasn't sure.

He had felt a feeling similar to this once when he had kissed Emma Rae Mallory when they were both fifteen years old.

They had snuck behind the stables and kissed and held hands one day when his mother was giving one of her fancy parties.

Although he had a lot of worries, he was free to plan his future.

Although he didn't know what the future held, he did know that horses were in his future.

As he broke camp, he thought about all he had heard said about the wild horses. To tell the truth, the only wild horses he had seen were in the area between the settlement and Santa Fe. He had seen them grazing in the distance on both sides of the trail.

The plan that involved more than one rider running the horses down, was out of the question. He was by himself.

But what about the second plan? The one the man had mentioned of building a corral near where the horses went for water. That might be a plan that one man could manage.

He'd have to search out the canyons and scout out where the horses lived, and where they went to drink.

And he'd need a house before the winter.

But what about money?

He needed a few things, like an axe and a saw, and food. He needed a job to get money for these things.

As he rode over the crest of the trail leading down into the canyon, he thought of the woman at the mine who had asked him to pick up the rock for her. They had almost gotten into a squabble, but she *had* asked him if he was interested in a job.

Maybe he was. He'd try anything once, even mining. Maybe he'd go there first. Hire on for a while. Get some money and then follow his dream about the wild horses.

He had enough food so that he could scout out the horse canyons, first, before he went to the mine.

He needed to do that, to see if his dream was practical. If it wasn't going to be practical, he needed to know that first, so he could make other plans.

He enjoyed the ride down the steep canyon trail. He was careful to keep his mind on what he was doing, and not get lost in thought. Blacky was alert and careful, also.

At the bottom, he rode the trail along the creek, and he and Blacky stopped to enjoy the clear, cold, fresh running water. Tom filled his canteens.

As they rode out of the entrance to the canyon, Tom went over in his head what the prospector had told him about where the wild horse canyons were. Two were near south of Lame Horse Canyon. Tom decided to try the nearest one first.

As night fell, he was near the entrance to the first canyon that the prospector had described. Tom hadn't seen any horses yet, but he saw horse manure.

It gave him confidence in what the prospector had said.

He was happy as he made camp for the night, careful to move a few hundred feet away from the trail that indicated that livestock of some kind traveled through here on a regular basis.

In the morning, he located the herd and watched them, hidden, from a distance.

Over the next week and a half, Tom studied the stallion of the group of wild horses.

The stallion was a gentleman. He was gallant in the way he protected his herd. He always drank last. He kept watch while the foals and the mares drank. He led the group to places of refuge when he felt that danger threatened.

He always placed himself between them and danger.

Yet Tom also saw this magnificent creature play in the creek water like a carefree child.

This particular stallion was brown, with a battle scar on his left haunch from a previous encounter with some danger; either another stallion, man, or mountain lion. Tom had no way of knowing. But it did look like it had been made by a hoof of some kind. It was a jagged semicircle, and looked like it had been a long time healing.

When he left the first canyon, he scouted out the second band of wild horses, and was reassured to find a large group. There were other canyons around he would check out later.

He would be careful to only capture a few horses at a time to tame, so that each group would have enough mares left to reproduce.

Then he was on his way to the mine. As he rode,

he thought about whether to build a house in Lame Horse Canyon, or in Paradise Canyon.

Paradise Canyon, he decided. With a large sign at the entrance to it, officially naming it Paradise Canyon.

Chapter Twenty-one

It was just after dawn as he approached the mine. He heard voices. At first, he was not paying too much attention, but as he rode over the last crest, he was surprised at who he saw working next to the woman.

It was Jake Jameson! Jameson was still working for June Webster the last time he had seen him.

As he rode up within ten feet of Jake, he was very blunt; partially because of his surprise.

"Jake!" Tom said, as he dismounted. "What in blazes are you doing here? I thought you were going to stay on and help Miss Webster."

Jake looked over toward the same woman that Tom had talked to the first time he had come to this mine. Jameson looked ashamed, but defensive.

"Hello," the woman said. She was dressed much in the same way she was the first time Tom had seen her. She ignored what Tom had said to Jake and began her own conversation with Tom as if Jake weren't there.

"How'd everything work out? Did you find your brother?" she asked.

"I'm right glad to tell you that you were right that day. My brother *was* working for the Zeigler mine. Everything is all straightened out, and he's gone back east, home."

"Glad to hear that. You know where the water is, if you need it," she said.

"Thanks," Tom said.

Tom turned his attention back to Jake.

"What happened?"

Jake looked kind of hangdog.

"Harry Webster died, did you know that?" Jake said, trying to change the subject.

"No. I hadn't heard. Sorry about that."

"When?"

"Coupla days after you left."

Again, Tom tried to find out why Jake was here.

"What happened? Why did you leave? I kind of thought that you and Miss Webster..."

Jake looked surprised. Then he looked guiltily over at the woman, who was listening attentively, and Tom suddenly realized that Jake and this woman might be romancing each other. The woman gave Jake a piercing glance and then said in a bossy way, "Jake, go get that wheelbarrow of ore and bring it over here."

"Sure, Connie," Jake said.

Jake seemed only too eager to escape. He walked over to where a wheelbarrow stood outside of the mine entrance, loaded with ore.

The mine seemed to be doing well. There were wagons full of copper ore waiting to be driven to stampers.

And voices coming from a large, new shack where breakfast was apparently being served to additional hired men.

Fifteen or twenty large gray and brown mules were in a corral on the right.

As Jake scurried gratefully away, the woman spoke.

"Jake fell off the wagon after you left. Seems he and June Webster had some kind of a deal about his not drinking while he was there.

"On top of that, he was horrified to find out that she was planning to raise peaches in the canyon, not have a ranch. He didn't like that. She bought little peach trees from local Indians. She was checking into raising apple and pear trees."

She put her hands on her hips and spoke bluntly. "I have one advantage over June Webster. As far as I'm concerned, what Jake does on his own time is his own dang business. You have to understand one thing about Jake. The bottom line is that Jake takes care of Jake first," the woman said.

"Who is with her now?" Tom asked. "Who is helping her? Did Jake leave her all alone?"

"Yes."

Tom turned his horse.

"You're not staying for breakfast?" the woman asked.

"Just a drink of water, ma'am, and I'll be on my way," Tom said. "Thanks."

He led Blacky to the seep, and came back to where the woman and Jake stood.

Jake avoided looking Tom in the eye.

Evidently she still looked for gold hidden in the rocks that had quartz in them.

As he put the next piece of quartz ore on the board for the woman to crush, Jake said to Tom, "Wasn't no use me waitin' around. It was you she had her eye on all the time."

"Me?" Tom said. "She scarcely spoke to me. It was you she spoke to every night after supper."

"She was just tellin' me what it was she wanted us to do; how she wanted the house built!" Jake shrugged. "Don't make no matter who she spoke to. After you left, I could tell she felt quite bad. Cried a little. Was quite upset that you had left. She loved her brother. An' they had come out west to try to get him better. Well, I don't need to say no more in front of a lady. But it was you she was after. I don't know how you could have thought she liked me. I'm not good enough . . . well, as I said, I don't need to say no more."

He stopped, noticing that the woman had stopped pounding and was listening.

"Thanks for the water and for the information." Tom tipped his hat to the woman, nodded curtly to Jake, and left.

How could Jake have left her all alone like that!

He turned Blacky and rode on out of sight of the mine. Soon he was back on the trail to where her little house was in Lame Horse Canyon.

All his own plans would have to be put on hold.

He had to make sure that June Webster was all right.

"Blacky, I'm sorry. I thought you were going to get

Casey's Journey

some rest while I worked in the mine. But I guess that's not going to happen."

Now he was in a hurry, and for the first time, cursed the great distances that he had so loved before.

He was relieved when the red rocks came into view once again.

In his mind he calculated the distance to the wild horse canyons and how long it would take to go back and forth between Lame Horse Canyon and where the wild horses were.

Not too long a distance.

He had to stop once and let Blacky "blow," and he realized that he had better slow down. Blacky had a lot of heart, but they had been on a long journey. Once he had some of the wild horses trained, he could give Blacky a well-deserved rest once in a while.

He was relieved when he rode into the entrance to Lame Horse Canyon.

It was late afternoon.

Some tiny peach trees were planted in neat rows on both sides of the small road leading off the main trail and down to the Websters' house.

He rode toward the small house he had helped build. It was set back from the creek.

June Webster must have heard the noise of Blacky's hooves because she appeared in the doorway of the little house.

"Mr. Casey!" she said, hurrying out to meet him, as Tom rode up close to the house and dismounted. "Mr. Casey, I'm so glad to see you!"

"So am I. I mean, I'm glad to see you, too," Tom said. What he wanted to do was to stop this pretense of politeness and take her in his arms and kiss her. But he worried that what Jake had said was wrong.

He knew the way he'd felt about her since the first day he'd seen her.

But her brother had died since he'd seen her last, and Jake had failed her. She'd had a lot of troubles since he'd ridden off to Santa Fe.

But Jake had said . . .

He was torn. He didn't know just what to do.

She solved the problem somewhat. Instead of putting out her hand to shake his, she pulled him to her and hugged him close.

Surprised, he was not so surprised that he didn't know enough to hug her back. He was bold enough to put his head down gently on the top of her head below him, on his chest.

"I'm so glad you're back," she said in a muffled voice. "Jake—"

"I know. I saw Jake. He's over at a copper mine a few hours from here.

"He—"

"I know."

"Do you know everything?" she said, pulling back a bit and looking up at him in a teasing, flirtatious way.

"No. There's lots I don't know."

"Do you know, then, how I feel about you?"

"No, but I was hoping . . ." he said.

"Hoping for what?"

"Hoping . . . for the best." he said.

"What would the best be?" she said, still teasing.

He was encouraged by the fact that she was still holding on to him, gently but firmly.

"I guess that you would feel about me the way I feel about you."

"And that is . . ."

"Are you going to make me actually come right out and say it? Right here?"

"Yes." she said.

"That I love you?"

"Yes."

"All right. I love you. And if the truth be told, I have since the first day I saw you with your wagon overturned on the road."

He could feel his face reddening. "I'm sorry. I shouldn't have said that, what with your recent bereavement, and all."

"It's all right. Harry and I knew for a long time that he was going to die. We had come out here for his health, but it didn't help. And he was worried about what would become of me after he died. That's why he hung on so long, even though he was in a lot of pain.

"We never mentioned it, but I think he knew I found you attractive, and I think he was glad. It gave him a kind of peace before he died. That's the kind of man he was.

"He saw how respectful you were of us both. He appreciated that. Harry was a good, kind man. The last couple of days, he simply slept all the time. He was never conscious.

"He never knew that you left. And we can take our time. We have the rest of our lives." She leaned in and hugged him again. "I'm so happy to see you. I'm so happy you came back."

Lame Horse Canyon, with its beautiful red rock walls, isn't such a bad place to live, if that's what she wants, he thought to himself. They could talk it over later.

As she looked up, he found the courage to lean down and kiss her.

"How do you feel about raising horses?" he asked, when he removed his lips from hers for a moment only, intending to lean down and kiss her again as soon as she answered.

"I've heard that horses like to eat apples," she said, smiling. She pointed to some small apple trees she had planted in neat lines in a cleared field on a bench up from the creekbed.

"I've heard they do, too," Tom said.

They both laughed joyfully as behind them, Blacky snorted his agreement.

BERTHA BARTLETT PUBLIC LIBRARY
503 Broad St.
Story City, IA 50248